Elvis Is Alive

Robert Mickey Maughon, M.D.

© 1997 Robert Mickey Maughon, M.D. & Cinnamon Moon™
All rights reserved under International and Pan-American Copyright Conventions. Published in the United States by Cinnamon Moon Publishing.
Library of Congress Catalog Number: LCCN 97-65727 ISBN: 0-9650366-2-6
Cover Art by Claudia Williams of Williams Design Nashville, TN
Text layout by WORDWIZ of Sevierville, TN
Printed in Nashville by Vaughan Printing

FOREWORD

Elvis Presley is unique among the world's entertainers. Never before has a performer been kept "alive" by his legions of fans as Elvis has.

This novel is a look at Elvis Presley's unique place in history and his seeming immortality. We hope that his family and his millions of fans will appreciate this novel for what it is, a "tongue in cheek" look at the phenomenon that is Elvis.

ELVIS IS ALIVE is a work of fiction. The Elvis Presley Estate has not sanctioned this book.

The Editors

*This novel is dedicated to my beautiful wife
Donna Marie Maughon.*

Chapter One

I saw him pass ghostlike through the misty fog rolling off the Seine. A streetlight outlined him eerily. He glided straight toward me on the cobblestone side street. I squinted and held my hand above my brow, attempting to attain a clearer view through the mist. He walked past a small bar whose flashing red neon light illuminated him. Suddenly, the combination of the two lights cast a halo around his head. I startled at the image.

I had searched for him the past year of my life. Now, here in Paris, I was apparently going to meet him.

When he got within ten yards of me, he began to extend his hand.

"Are you Dr. St. John?" he asked while firmly gripping my hand.

"Yes, I am," I stammered in reply, still shielding my eyes from the brightly illuminated figure standing before me.

"Good to meet you," he said. "I'm Elvis Presley."

"Let's go into the bar," I said, pointing toward the establishment he had just passed.

We both turned and entered the small Parisian bar identical to hundreds of others in the city.

There was only an old man smoking a strong

French cigarette standing behind the worn oaken bar.

"*Parlez-vous Anglais?*" I asked the old man.

"*Oui*, yes," he responded, knocking ashes from the glowing tobacco. "Sit down," he said in a thick French accent. He pointed toward a table by a small window and brought us a list of drinks.

I asked for coffee, black. The stranger who said he was Elvis Presley surveyed the menu.

He was slim. He looked younger than he had twenty years earlier. The bloated Elvis was gone. His beautiful dark skin had not aged. His jet black hair had not grayed.

He did have a sneer in that lip.

I watched him and was still somewhat skeptical that this was actually Elvis Aron Presley.

I had met so many convincing impostors over the past year. I had prepared myself for still another letdown tonight. Then, as he ordered an obscure African coffee from the bartender, something caught my eye: his hands.

You can change facial features through surgery. Ears, noses, chins, even buttocks can be altered. You can also change fingerprints, but you cannot modify the basic structure of the hands. As a doctor, and an Elvis fan from childhood, I instantly realized that this indeed was the one and only true Elvis Presley. It was his hands that gave him away.

I felt a tear form in my eye. He noticed it as he handed the menu back to the Frenchman and gently reached over and touched my hand.

"Are you okay?"

"Yes, yes, I am," I said as I wiped my eyes. "It's just that I really know that it's you." I shook my head, unable to continue.

He simply gripped the top of my hand in reassurance and patiently waited for me to speak.

Regaining my composure, I said slowly, "There are so many things I want to ask you."

He nodded in understanding.

The bartender crossed the floor with Elvis' coffee. Elvis held his hand out as if to halt me.

"First you have to do one thing for me, Dr. St. John."

Leaning back in my chair, I replied, "Yes, sure, anything."

"Tell me how you found me and..."

"I see, I see," I interrupted. "That's quite fair." I gathered my thoughts, continuing to nod in agreement. As I sipped my coffee, I offered, "If I tell you how I came here to find you in Paris, Mr. Presley—"

"Elvis, please," he interrupted. "No one has ever called me Mr. Presley."

"Okay, if I tell you about the journey to find you, will you explain everything about—" I halted in mid-sentence.

He simply stared at me with those eyes. A laughing young French couple passed outside the window. They were oblivious to the astounding revelation that was unfolding in this nondescript French café.

I continued, "Will you tell me why you're here, still alive, when in 1977 you supposedly died?"

There. I had blurted it out. A faint smile seemed to play over his face. He didn't say anything for a long time. Finally, he spoke. "I won't promise you anything," was all he said. He paused, and after what seemed to be an eternity, he slowly continued, "but all I will say is that I am willing to listen and then we will see."

I started to speak when he interrupted, "Yeah, sure. Why not? You're from Tennessee, aren't you? I'll give a fellow Tennessean a break." He smiled, noticing my curious expression. "I could tell by your accent. That's why I'm here with you tonight. You've certainly gotten closer than anyone else."

"Okay," I said in agreement. "I'll tell you my story first, and then we'll go from there."

I sighed deeply. "Where should I begin?" I asked as I gazed out the window into the foggy Paris night.

I began by telling him a little about my background. He seemed genuinely interested. I described my medical training in New Orleans and complications that had arisen there. I then explained how I had met my wife and lost her in a tragic way. That brought me to the reason I started my search for him in the beginning. He leaned slightly forward in a manner that seemed to display an "I'm listening" attitude.

I continued with the story of my acceptance of the coroner's job in Memphis—how after losing my wife Betsy, I had felt as if I had nothing else to lose. I explained how I had thought the coroner's position would be an easy, uncomplicated job.

I shook my head and said, "Boy, was that ever a miscalculation."

He smiled broadly. "Explain, I'm curious."

I smiled and asked, "Are you sure?"

"Yes, I'm sure. In a way this is going to be therapy for me," he reasoned. "It interests me to find out what would drive a man to follow a ghost around the world for a year of his life."

His statement shocked me back to reality. I imagine if one didn't know the whole story of my quest, it would appear to be absurd. Even now I have to remind myself of the reality of the story or it would seem to be a farce.

"Before I start, do you want another cup of coffee?" I asked.

"Sure, that sounds great." He motioned for the old man and pointed to the empty cups signaling for a refill.

"I love good coffee, do you?" he asked.

"Yes, I do. It actually seems to make me relax despite the caffeine. I especially like a cup before entertaining," he said.

"Entertain?" I asked. "Where? You mean now?"

"Whoa, not so fast, Dr. St. John. You promised to tell your story first, remember?" He held his hands up in protest.

"Okay, okay, that was the deal." I said, smiling.

The bartender brought the steaming liquid over and poured it into our cups. Elvis thanked the gentleman and turned his attention back to me.

"Go on. You were saying..."

"I think I'll start when I moved to Memphis."

"Good idea," he remarked. "It's always best to start from the beginning. He smiled and shifted in his chair to get more comfortable. "Go on, I'm listening."

Robert Mickey Maughon, M.D.

Chapter Two

I began by explaining how I had decided to interview for the Memphis opening.

"I had learned about the position through a friend of mine. She called me when I was in Hawaii, knowing that I wanted to return home to be closer to my sister. The thought of being a medical coroner had never really crossed my mind. The job didn't really pay that well and wasn't what I had been trained to do, but after the interview I decided if they offered me the job, I'd accept it. It would accomplish my goal of getting closer to home. I have to admit that even though I'd gone to medical school in Memphis, the thought of returning to that town really didn't appeal to me."

"You don't like Memphis?" he interrupted.

"No, that's not what I mean," I started to explain. "Even though Memphis is in Tennessee, it's still a long way from Knoxville, which is home. It really didn't get me that much closer to my sister. So you see, it has nothing to do with Memphis, it's more a matter of distance."

"Yeah, it really is a long state, isn't it?"

"Yes, it is," I replied. "I hated making that drive across the state."

"I see" was all he said.

Elvis Is Alive

Steam wafted above the coffee cups. I completely forgot my one-man audience as I remembered the day I had interviewed for the coroner's position. Soon I had taken myself back in time to Memphis. I began to remember and relay my story.

* * * * *

"Dr. St. John!" came the voice from the corridor of the Memphis Airport. "I'm Dr. Regent. Welcome back to Tennessee."

"Nice to meet you, Dr. Regent," I said as we shook hands.

"Let me take your bag," the older gentleman offered.

"No, that's okay. I've got it. What's new in Memphis?" I asked, making small talk.

"Oh, nothing really. I was just trying to decide where we should go to dinner to discuss the position. We have a new barbecue joint out west that has made a big splash," the gray-haired man said.

"Barbecue will always be big here. It's a staple in the diet of the good citizens, as I recall," I said.

"Unfortunately, that's correct," Dr. Regent noted. "And if you accept this position, you will dissect the clogged arteries that the porcine concoction precipitates." The older physician followed his exaggerated description of the tangy ribs and the disease it causes with, "but it sure is delightful going down!" His relaxed manner immediately put me at ease.

"Is this new restaurant better than the Rendezvous downtown?" I asked.

"I don't think so, but it's pretty damn tasty."

"Let's go then," I offered.

The restaurant, Bones, catered to mostly affluent East Memphians: people who should have known better than to indulge in the most fat- and cholesterol-laden food ever invented. It was a boisterous crowd that crammed into every corner of the place.

* * * * *

"Boy, I sure do miss good "Q."

The voice of Elvis Presley expressing his affection for this most Southern of foods jolted me back to the present in Paris.

"I liked fried peanut butter and banana sandwiches better," Elvis' voice trailed off.

"Look, do you mind if I order something...more...medicinal," I whispered, noticing my hands trembling. The enormity of the situation had finally struck me.

"Sure. I would join you," Elvis offered, "but I don't drink. No matter what else I did, I never did drink."

Feeling my face flush with embarrassment, I stammered "I...I...wasn't implying anything."

"Forget it," he said. "All of that other crap was always kind of overblown anyway."

I waved for the old man and attempted to point to a bottle of Jack Daniel's behind the bar. Elvis interrupted me.

"I bet it isn't!" he said.

"What isn't?" I asked, still trying to direct the barkeep to the black-labeled bottle on the back shelf.

"The 'Q' from that new restaurant can't be as

good as old Charlie Vargas's Rendezvous downtown."

"Well no, I didn't think it was quite as good," I said. In reality, I couldn't remember what I had eaten there.

The French bartender finally brought me my favorite alcoholic beverage, Jack on the rocks. I must have had a curious look on my face because Elvis took a long sip of coffee, smiled and shrugged: "I just like barbecue. Go ahead," he encouraged, taking another sip. "This is really taking me back home."

I smiled. I was glad I had given him a positive remembrance of his former life.

"Where was I?"

"You and the other doctor were going out to eat. You were going to discuss the job."

"That's right," I said, taking a sip of my drink. I began to recant the happenings of that evening in Memphis that would change the course of my life and send me in search of the man who now sat in front of me.

* * * * *

"Dr. St. John, this job will be a piece of cake for you," Dr. Regent was speaking with his mouth full, "if you know pathology, which with your background, you should." His rib bib rustled with every word. At Bones, customers were provided with a big bib much like those in New England lobster pots. The reason here, of course, was to prevent barbecue sauce, instead of lobster juice, from spoiling clothing.

"I never thought about doing anything like this,

Dr. Regent," I explained. "But it will be a way for me to be closer to my sister."

"We want you for the job," Dr. Regent interrupted. "To be blunt, the medical examiner's job is not one that is very lucrative, so even though you think you're not qualified, we think you would be a great addition. Remember, this job will also require you to teach at the medical units."

"Really?" I asked. "That's great. I've always wanted to teach."

"We at the University have always felt that experience such as yours is a valuable adjunct to the person who takes this job. Besides, I'll be honest, nobody wants to take these jobs anymore." Dr. Regent looked at me straight in the eye. "If you want a clean job, good benefits, and normal hours, then this position is not for you because of the poor salary and irregular hours. You're always up at two a.m. to look at some corpse..." his voice tailed off. Looking up from his plate, he continued, "There I've said it! The truth!"

"So...are you offering me the job?"

"Well, yes, I am. Of course, final approval rests with the board at the hospital and the county commission. But I can assure you that all of that is just a formality." Dr. Regent said, beaming.

I smiled back. Nonchalantly, I asked, "Is it really that hard to fill these positions? Surely it's not that bad."

Dr. Regent cleared his throat. "Well, now that you've taken the job..." With that statement, he began to reiterate all the negatives. I drifted off as he droned on. In reality, I hadn't signed a contract yet, so I could get out of this arrangement if it was really horrible. The only real reasons that I decided to take the job were that it placed me closer to home and I would be able to teach at the medical center. I had always pictured myself as a professor in a university somewhere. This is probably the closest I would get. I had only worked emergency room jobs in my career. I had never been in private practice, and therefore I had never made any major money. Money really wasn't that big of a deal to me. The odd hours that Dr. Regent mentioned weren't a problem either. Hell, I had been an ER doc, for Pete's sake. I knew what screwy hours were like. I had studied pathology in my last residency. I was ready!

"The bodies that are decomposed..." he continued. He paused and looked at my plate. His face turned slightly red. "Sorry, I forgot we were at the dinner table."

"Tell me about the teaching," I said. "I think I can handle everything, even the decomposing bodies."

"Ah," he said in an all-knowing way. "It appears the good doctor wants to be a professor."

"Well, I..." His statement had caught me off guard for some reason.

"Yes, I must say that the thought of teaching appeals to me. I never thought I would be in a situation, other than teaching an occasional student in the ER, to do any real teaching. The teaching aspect really does appeal to me."

Dr. Regent realized he had hit a hot button with me. He began to gush. "Oh yes, you'll teach at least two days a week! The school will ask you to come in and discuss the case of the week and explain any pathology, but mainly teach the associated anatomy. To be quite honest, it's an inexpensive way to have a class in forensics." He shrugged his shoulders and said simply, "Budget cuts."

I smiled as he returned to the job of eating his dinner. That bib tied around his neck made him look rather silly. I suppressed a small chuckle, releasing it outwardly as a smile. I imagined myself standing in front of a class of medical students, boldly explaining the latest Memphis murder, and how I, through careful investigation of the evidence gathered at autopsy, had solved the case.

"Good then," he gave me a hard pat on the back. "I'll tell the commission that we have our man." Dr. Regent extended his hand over the plate of discarded ribs and asked, "Do we have a deal?"

"Yes, I guess we do."

* * * * *

"So, then you even taking the job was a kind of fluke, huh?" Elvis' voice jolted me back to the present.

"Sorry," he continued, noticing I'd been lost in the past.

"Yeah, yeah, it really was. It was one of those fluky things," I agreed.

"Kind of like me being the 'king of rock 'n' roll'!" he interjected.

"Bartender," he waved at the old man. Getting his attention, he pointed to his cup. Turning to me, he asked, "Are you ready for another one?"

"Sure," I said. The look on my face must have invited an explanation. After getting the bartender's attention and placing the order, he turned back to me and continued.

"Well, think about it," he offered. "A poor, shy,

Southern boy who loves to sing, becomes the 'king of rock 'n' roll.'" The old bartender poured the coffee for him and sat down my drink.

Taking a sip from the cup, he continued: "What are the odds of one person making an impact like that? It was all timing." His eyes drifted above mine. He looked blankly at the wall, then added, "It's amazing how things turn out sometimes, isn't it?"

I got the feeling he was expressing his opinion more for himself than for me. "Yes it really is, isn't it?" I added as I swirled my drink.

"What...what? Excuse me," he said.

"I was confirming what you just said, that it's amazing how things can turn out sometimes."

"Sorry. I guess I was allowing myself a bit of nostalgia." He smiled and his eyes lost the glazed look that had drifted over them. For several minutes, we sat there and allowed each other time to reminisce about the twists and turns of our lives.

The night had dragged on. It actually had become quite late. The old Frenchman didn't seem to mind. If he did, he didn't say anything as he continued to smoke cigarette after cigarette. The smoke silently floated around the small bar in cloud-like layers. I suddenly began to feel as if I were in a surreal world. Here I was, having a conversation with a man who had supposedly been dead for the last twenty years.

Suddenly I felt a wave of dizziness. It seemed to descend from the ceiling of the smoke-filled room. I shook my head in an effort to regain some semblance of reality.

"Hey, are you okay, Dr. St. John?" The legendary compassion of this man was evident in his voice.

"Yes. It's been a long day, that's all."

"Let's call it a night then," he offered.

"No, no," I protested quickly. The thought of his walking out of my life now after my long search brought me back to a normal, albeit panicked, state of mind.

"Don't worry," he said, sensing my concern. "We'll meet here at the same time tomorrow night."

"Don't you want me to go with you?" I stammered.

Elvis laughed out loud. "I'm really enjoying this. This is good. Are you going to take care of the tab?" He stood to head back out into the Paris night.

"Oh, absolutely." I jumped up so hurriedly that I knocked my chair all the way to the wall behind me. The resulting crash startled the old bartender. His cigarette fell from his mouth as he yelled *"Mon Dieu!"*

"Sorry," I tried to apologize.

Elvis laughed quietly and offered his hand.

"It's been great meeting you."

I took his hand and shook it. His handshake was firm and reassuring, more sincere and longer in duration than normal. It was a Southern handshake.

"I'll see you tomorrow night then. Same time." I simply nodded and repeated, "Same time."

With that he walked out the door. He passed in front of the window, raised his hand and waved as if to say, "See you tomorrow."

I watched him walk into the night, the thickening mist and fog slowly enveloping him. I stared at the spot where he had been, longing to get another glimpse. The Paris night refused to cooperate.

"Monsieur." The old man had walked up to the table with the bill.

"Do you know who that is?" I asked the craggy-faced man.

"Who?" the old fellow answered, struggling with his English. He looked out into the darkness, his head bobbing up and down in an effort to try to catch a glimpse of my acquaintance.

"Never mind," I mumbled as I took the check from his hand. I paid him and said that we would be back at the same time the next evening. He shrugged his shoulders and in a strong French accent said, "Okay."

Chapter Three

The same fog that had swallowed Elvis now clung stickily to me. I meandered down the street toward my hotel, La Parisian, on the Rue Fleur. I had to get the security guard to let me in. The Belgian cuckoo clock on the wall next to my room revealed that it was three a.m.

No wonder the guy looked perturbed when he let me back in, I mused. The courtyarded old Paris hotel had seen its better days. It had been a haven for beatniks and other "cool" people back in the sixties. I had taken a room there because it was affordable, available, and clean. The locked gate made it feel safe. Maybe safety was an American concern, but the gate reassured me.

After I entered my room, I sat down on the single bed against the wall. I immediately began to calculate the time back in Memphis. I felt a compulsion to call Marcia. She and I had met when I first began to teach at the medical school. Aside from being my lover, she had supported my decision to follow my heart and attempt to find Elvis Presley. Others thought I was nuts, but not Marcia Redmon. She said, "Go for it."

Forgetting that modern technologies had largely corrected the aggravating mess that used to be the French national telephone system, I almost didn't call because I didn't want the hassle. After staring at the ceiling from my bed for an indeterminate amount of time, I picked up the receiver and dialed home.

"Hello." Marcia's voice was faint but distinct. "Robert, is that you?"

"Marcia," I interrupted. "Guess what!"

"Are you okay, Robert?"

"Yes, I'm fine...perfect. Marcia, I've found him. I've found..." my voice trailed off, "Elvis."

A long pause followed. "Are you sure?"

"Yes, yes, I'm sure. There's no doubt about it. I just talked with him tonight for several hours, and yes, he's alive and well. There is absolutely no doubt about it."

"Congratulations! I can't wait to tell everyone!" she continued.

"Not yet, Marcia. I want to get a better understanding of everything."

"Are you sure? I'm so excited. You're positive it's him?"

"Positive. I think it's best though, if we keep this to ourselves for right now. Listen, I'm exhausted. It's three a.m. in Paris. I'll call you back tomorrow or the next day, okay?"

"Was it worth it? You know, all the time and effort?"

"I don't know yet. It's pretty strange..."

"Yes, I can imagine. Listen, do you...will you get the money?"

"I don't know that either. It's late. I really need to get some sleep."

"Okay, Robert. Be careful and be sure to keep me posted."

"I will. Good night." I was so exhausted, I don't remember hanging up the telephone.

I didn't awaken the next day until around noon. I immediately felt a sense of urgency as I waited for night to arrive so we could continue our conversation. I had been in Paris for only forty-eight hours. I felt a tourist's twinge to visit all the sights.

I was overtaken instead by the need to categorize all my thoughts and questions about him. I put the details of my entire journey to find him in a mental list. The idea of taking a written list with me tonight was out of the question. But I had agreed, after all, to detail my efforts to find him before he answered any of my questions, so I needed to make a good mental picture of everything in order to hear his story more quickly. By the time I had planned the evening's conversation, it was twilight. I ate a small meal at the hotel and then decided to get an early start to the bar. I wanted to make sure we had the same table as the previous evening. I felt it would make us more comfortable.

When I arrived, the same old bartender greeted me at the entrance with an acknowledgment in the form of a smile. He waved graciously to the table that we had occupied the previous evening. The bar was empty again. It was little wonder the old gentleman was so accommodating with the business this place did. He needed every customer he could get.

I hadn't really taken in the establishment the previous evening. I took a few minutes to visually explore it. Behind the bar were rows upon rows of liquor and wooden racks of wine. If one stepped

Elvis Is Alive

outside the front door, turned on tiptoes and looked above the facade of the old building, the illuminated tip of the Eiffel Tower could be seen.

I had begun to accept the toothless but amiable French barkeep as part of the furniture. I glanced up at the bar. Sure enough, the ever-present cigarette was oscillating from his lips. I began to count the layers of smoke that seemingly billowed from it.

"Good evening." Elvis greeted me.

I literally jumped up, the words had startled me so.

"Good evening," I reciprocated, pushing myself away from the table. I shook his extended hand firmly. His smile was contagious. I instantly felt at ease.

"How are you enjoying your stay in Paris so far?" Elvis asked as he sat down in front of me. "Have you seen any of the sights yet?"

"The timing has not been good," was all I could muster.

"Let's get something from the bartender." Elvis waved for the old man. Instantly he shuffled to us and nodded his head up and down as an indication he was ready to take our order. That infernal cigarette continued to dangle from his lip.

"I want the same coffee I had last night," Elvis allowed.

"I think I'll try some also, if it's that good."

The old man grunted his understanding and shuffled off to the bar.

"It's that good!" Elvis said.

"So where did we leave off last night?" he asked.

"Hmm...let me think," I responded, not wanting to appear too anxious to get back to our conversation.

After all, I would have to go over some delicate matters in the course of our discussion. To be quite honest, it made me nervous. I was glad I had spent the day rehearsing what I was going to say and remembering the events of the past.

"Before we get started, I want to tell you that I told someone that I met with you and talked with you."

"Doesn't matter," Elvis smiled broadly. "They won't believe you anyway."

"Yes, she will," I responded. I had felt guilty about telling Marcia somehow.

"What did she say?" he asked curiously. I could tell he was interested by the way he leaned forward in his chair and stared at me intently with those piercing eyes.

"She said, 'Congratulations.'" I didn't dare let him know there was a monetary reward awaiting any person who could prove that Elvis Presley was alive. I felt that could be broached at a more appropriate time. I had just met him and was beginning to tell him about my journey; he hadn't even approached the subject of his extraordinary story. Besides, I knew how far I would get if I suggested that he go public about his existence. I adjusted my chair and cleared my throat.

"She was happy. She's a nice girl." I shrugged.

"And she believed you?" He looked incredulous.

"Yes, she did. Why wouldn't she?"

He laughed. "Well," he waved his hands in front of his face, "after all..."

"Oh yeah, that." I couldn't help but chuckle a little myself. "No, she believes me." I tried to play it down. I didn't want to get into the monetary aspect of my beginning to search for him.

In reality, the financial reward had faded into

the background as I followed this icon around the world. My journey had come to mean much more to me than a few dollars.

"I just wanted to let you know, you know...to be honest...that I had told someone about you."

He shook his head slightly and said, "No, that's okay."

I changed the subject. "I was telling you about how I took the medical examiner's job in Memphis."

"That's right. Go ahead. You were telling me about you and Dr. Regent."

"We were having supper at Bones."

"Yes, that's right. I remember because it reminded me of the barbecue back home as a kid."

"Where did I leave off?"

"You were at the point where you took the job."

"Pardon, s'il vous plait," the bartender stuck the brightly colored coffee cups in front of us.

Elvis looked up and smiled. *"Merci beaucoup."*

"Merci." The old man meandered back to his permanent station at the bar.

"Yeah, I think I had just taken the job." I felt myself sliding back in time as I translated the story.

* * * * *

"It's set then Dr. St. John. You start next month," Dr. Regent said.

"Okay, but I need to find a place to live."

"No problem, my boy! We'll set you up in an apartment in midtown Memphis. They're affiliated with the University, and the rent will be reasonable."

"I'll get that," he interrupted himself as the waitress brought the check to the table.

"I'll at least pay my share," I offered.

"Nonsense, my boy, picking up the tab is just part of my job." Dr. Regent laughed heartily. "I'm glad to do it."

After paying the bill, we passed the bar and left the restaurant.

We went to the parking lot and found our cars. Before we parted, Dr. Regent said, "Why don't you come by the office tomorrow and we'll sign the contract?"

"Sure...why not...sounds good to me," I replied.

"Good, it's settled. I'll see you around ten a.m. then."

"Okay, Dr. Regent, I'll see you in the morning."

We shook hands. As he was leaving, he looked back over his shoulder and offered, "Good having you on board, doctor. I look forward to seeing you in the morning."

* * * * *

"So you took the job without even asking how much money you'd make?" Elvis interrupted.

I jumped a bit. "Yeah, I forgot to mention that. Sorry, I get so lost in my story that I forget myself sometimes."

"That's okay, Dr. St. John, you're a good storyteller. I'm enjoying your saga."

I took a long sip of coffee and smiled. He likes my story, I thought. Good, I'm making progress then.

"Go on, what happened the next day? I'm curious."

"Hmmm...let me see...let me see if I can remember." I was really beginning to enjoy myself.

* * * * *

"Good morning, Dr. St. John," Dr. Regent welcomed me as his secretary showed me into his office.

The medical school was located in downtown Memphis. The medical examiner's office had been incorporated into the medical school in order to save money. As I entered the office, I was picturing myself as a joint teacher and "medical sleuth." Dr. Regent followed me into the room. On the cherry-paneled walls were an assortment of trophies: stuffed exotic animal heads, fish, footballs, baseballs, and other plaques. It was a virtual museum or, better said, a memorabilia wall of awards and mementoes of his past.

"Do you like it?" he asked.

"Yeah, I do," I answered as I continued to look up and around the room in amazement. The skin of a huge rattlesnake with gigantic fangs displayed in an obvious attempt to impress the viewer caught my eye.

"That's the scariest dead thing I have ever seen," I commented.

Dr. Regent rolled back in his large overstuffed chair and put his hands behind his head. His silvery gray hair was tousled some as he placed his hands on top of his head and interlocked his fingers.

"Yeah, I killed that big fellow down the other side of El Paso, Texas. We were hunting mule deer. The guide said it was the biggest diamondback he had ever seen. Son of a gun was twelve feet long. Can you believe how big he stretches there in the middle?

"That big fellow had enough venom in one bite to kill an elephant," Dr. Regent exclaimed.

I replied, "It's plenty scary to me. How'd you kill it, anyway?"

"With my bare hands," Dr. Regent roared in delight. He thrust his hands in front of him and waved them wildly.

I looked back in mock respect and disbelief.

"Just kidding. I shot it with my rifle, a 30-06. Killed him with one shot through the head. It was one heck of a shot, if I say so myself."

Suddenly a young woman in her late twenties came rolling through the office door and said, "Dr. Regent, I can't stand the interns any longer."

At that moment, Dr. Marcia Redmon walked right into my life.

Chapter Four

I looked at Elvis and asked, "Do you believe in love at first sight? I ask because I never thought I would ever really love again, in that special way, after the death of my wife, Betsy."

"Yes, I believe in it," he responded very slowly, cautiously, but without hesitation. "That's the way I felt about Priscilla."

I blushed as bright a shade of crimson as God makes.

"That's okay," he said, noticing my embarrassment. "I'm not offended. I know exactly how you feel, when a woman walks into your life...and you know you'll never feel the same way about another one."

Regaining my composure somewhat, I said, "I'm glad you understand, and I hope I didn't offend you."

"No, no...please continue."

"Garcon, garcon..." He pointed to our nearly empty cups. I leaned forward across the table somewhat.

"Well...in she walked, indignant, full of vibrant energy, long reddish-blonde hair cut at the shoulders. Big blue flashy eyes, seemingly connected to the longest pair of legs I had ever seen."

"Did she have large breasts?" Elvis quizzed.

"What?" I asked, taken aback somewhat, but laughing at the question.

"Well, you must know that I'm somewhat of a ladies' man," he beamed.

"Yes, yes...I know what you're saying. I had forgotten about your reputation."

"Yes, as a matter of fact, she is fairly well endowed. I don't guess she would mind me telling you."

"Sorry, I forgot myself." It was his turn to be embarrassed. It was funny to see the 'king of rock 'n' roll' turn red.

"No problem. I think Marcia would like to know that Elvis Presley was interested in her sex appeal."

We both had a good laugh as the cups were being refilled. Then I resumed my story.

* * * * *

"Dr. St. John, let me introduce you to Dr. Marcia Redmon." Dr. Regent said as he stood and presented the young lady to me. "She's our ER director here at the trauma center."

Marcia jerked around, startled because she hadn't seen me sitting in the large chair facing Dr. Regent.

"He won't bite you, dear, I promise," Dr. Regent said laughing.

"I'm sorry, gentlemen. I didn't know you were occupied, Dr. Regent. Please excuse me."

I immediately began to babble, "Oh, no. No problem. I'm Robert St. John. I've just taken the medical examiner's job. As an old ER director, I understand the despicable nature and ignorance of some interns."

Laughing, Marcia extended her hand and shook mine.

"I'm Marcia Redmon.... I'll come back at a more appropriate time, Dr. Regent."

Again I immediately interjected, "Don't mind me," as I continued to shake her hand.

She gently but firmly removed her hand from mine. "I'll come back later." She smiled broadly, her large blue eyes twinkling at both of us as she left the room and closed the door behind her.

"Something, isn't she?" Dr. Regent gushed before I could say anything.

Plopping down in the large chair, I replied, "Yes, she really is."

Dr. Regent continued, "She's been our ER director for the past year, and we're very proud of her. She's exceptionally motivated and does a great job for us, and she's extremely pleasing to look at also." He paused a moment, then said, "So it looks as though you're ready to take the job."

"Yes. Do I have to meet the county commission?"

He waved his right hand in the air above his head in a dismissing motion.

"No...well, actually, yes...you do, but it's only a formality, as they will act on my recommendation. You really don't need to worry if you want the job."

I nodded my head in approval.

"That settles it. Do you want the apartment in midtown then? I'll arrange it for you if you want it."

I responded, "I guess I do.... I mean I haven't seen it yet so...."

"It's in the same complex where Dr. Redmon lives," Dr. Regent said.

"I'll take it then. I mean...I'd be a fool not to," I stammered.

Dr. Regent laughed a hearty, guttural laugh.

"I thought that would make up your mind for you." He continued to laugh. "Mrs. Mason," Dr. Regent addressed his secretary over the intercom, "will you please come in here?"

Mrs. Mason, a woman in her early sixties, poked her head around the door.

"Yes sir?" she asked.

"Mrs. Mason, this is Dr. Robert St. John. He's our new forensics teacher, which means he also will be the county medical examiner."

Mrs. Mason walked over to me and shook my hand. I immediately felt that I would like her. We exchanged pleasantries, then Dr. Regent asked her if she would mind escorting me to the apartment. She said she was only too happy to accommodate me, smiling. As we were leaving, Dr. Regent reassured me again that the county commission would okay my hiring. Again he said it was merely a formality, taking obvious delight in his political power.

As we walked out, Dr. Regent yelled out after me, "Do you want to sign the contract now? I completely forgot to ask you."

"Why not," I replied. I walked back into his office where he handed me three sets of documents that were five pages each.

"By the way, how much does this job pay?" I asked.

Dr. Regent smiled. "I wondered when you would get down to the money. It's $78,000 to start. Then we'll renegotiate the contract next year."

"Okay, I'll sign up for a year's stint." I signed all

three of the documents in front of me and then caught up with Mrs. Mason in her office.

"I'm officially an employee now," I announced as we headed out down the hall together.

"Good, glad to have you on board," the little lady said.

Walking down the stairwell, I asked if we could stop by the ER on our way out. Mrs. Mason politely asked if I had met Dr. Redmon, smiling in a knowing manner. I nodded yes. She nodded also, as if to say, "I thought so."

The ER was relatively calm as we entered. Marcia was examining a young girl. She was busy looking in the five-year-old's ear when I walked up to her without her seeing me.

"Marcia," I began.

"You are going to scare me to death," she said after she had jumped back from the patient. "I didn't hear you coming."

"Sorry, I was just passing through the ER with Mrs. Mason and wanted to see if I could get you to have dinner with me tonight. After all, I'm new in town and all alone."

The little girl looked at Dr. Redmon and said, "Go ahead and go, Miss Marcia, he looks like he needs some company."

"Thank you, young lady," I said appreciatively. "I'm a doctor too, so if you ever need anything, you be sure to ask for me since you helped me out here today."

"I guess I have no choice then," Marcia responded.

"Good, I'll pick you up at seven o'clock then, okay?"

Marcia looked at her young patient. "What do

you think? Is that an acceptable time for a first date?"

The young girl nodded and said, "But no kissing on the first date."

Marcia and I both looked at each other.

"Great. I'll see you at seven," I said. "It looks like we're going to be neighbors anyway."

"Really? Is that so?"

"Yes, that's where Mrs. Mason and I are going right now. We're off to see an apartment in your complex."

"That sounds great. You'll like it there."

The little girl began to pull on Marcia's arm. "You can visit with him tonight, Doctor Marcia, but now you need to doctor my ear."

Marcia looked at me, smiling. "You heard the young lady. I've got to get back to work. I'll see you tonight." She pulled the otoscope back up to the girl's ear and began to look inside.

* * * * *

Elvis again startled me when he said, "It's getting late. Would you prefer that we continue tomorrow night?"

I felt panicked, sensing that I was losing his interest. I immediately began to apologize. "I'm sorry. I feel like I'm boring you and intruding on your time."

"No, that's not it at all. Actually, I've enjoyed this...only I am wondering how all this leads you to finding me. Don't get me wrong, I'm not bored, just curious."

"I'll speed up the story then, because all of this is pertinent to my finding you."

Elvis leaned back some in his chair and nodded his head slightly. "Then go ahead," he said. "I've got nothing but time. I only meant that we could continue later if you were tired."

Searching for the correct words, I began. "Well, I want you to know and understand the whole story if you're interested."

He smiled and said, "I'm certainly interested or I wouldn't be here. Maybe this would be a good stopping place, though. Would you be interested in seeing me at work?"

My heart immediately began to beat faster as I realized he was opening up to me. I had searched for him, hoping just to be able to speak with him, and now he was inviting me to join him at his work. This was exceeding my wildest expectations. Without hesitation, I answered excitedly, "Of course. Absolutely. Any time." I attempted to mask my excitement, but with little success. Curious and unable to contain myself any longer, I asked, "What do you do?"

Without hesitation he replied, "I'm an Elvis Presley impersonator."

I don't know when I have seen anyone laugh harder than he did at that moment in response to the look on my face. He laughed so loudly that the old Frenchman almost fell off his barstool.

"You should see the look on your face," he said as soon as he could talk coherently.

"I just never dreamed that you would be doing anything like that."

"Why not? It makes sense. I still love to entertain, and besides, where else would you hide a turnip but in a turnip patch?"

"What do you mean? I don't understand."

"I mean, if you were Elvis Presley, what better way to disappear than as Elvis Presley. Look around, there are probably thirty Elvis impersonators in Paris alone. Besides, the French are so blasé that even if someone recognized me they probably wouldn't say anything anyway."

I looked at the man in awe. I still didn't know why he had decided to disappear. I might never get him to tell me; but, those people who had told me that Elvis Presley was not a smart man were wrong. How ingenious. How perceptive he was to correctly and rightly realize that the French people would not be impressed with this American, no matter who he was!

"Well, have they?"

"Well have they what?"

"You know, recognized you?"

"No, well, I don't think so, but you know what, Dr. St. John? You never really can tell about the people here. They're so unimpressed by American pop culture that they might never let on."

"You're kidding me."

"Let me ask you something. Would you like to come and see me perform?"

"Absolutely."

"Then why don't we call it a night and resume our conversation tomorrow evening. You can see my show, and then I'll meet you backstage."

"Great, how or where do I find you?"

"There's a small theater called the Elvis Review about fifteen blocks down. The show starts at 11 o'clock, so why don't you come down then and watch me perform and we'll meet afterward?"

He seemed to enjoy my obvious enthusiasm and excitement about being able to see him perform.

Elvis pulled out a pass and told me if I presented it at the front door, I'd have no trouble getting in to see him. He then stood up and shook my hand.
"I'll see you tomorrow night then."
He was walking out the door when I called after him, "Do you mind if I tell Marcia?"
"No," he answered, putting his hands in the air and shrugging his shoulders. "Like I said before, I don't think anyone will really believe you anyway. So tell anyone that you want as far as I care."
I waved goodbye and nodded my head in understanding.
My heart began to pound again. This was almost too good to believe. I had found Elvis Presley, and he was very much ALIVE! Plus, he had seemed to enjoy my company. He was even beginning to feel like a friend. And to top it off, I was going to see him perform, and he had invited me to join him backstage. I took the last sip of my coffee and headed out the door in search of the closest telephone to call Marcia.
"*S'il vous plait,*" the old man said after a sizable attention-getting cough. He held the check between two fingers and waved it at me. His furry eyebrows were doing a little Groucho Marx dance to let me know he wanted to be paid. At first I thought he was signaling that he had recognized Elvis.
I struggled to pull some money from my pocket. Glancing over at him, I tried to get a better feel for the situation. If he had accidentally recognized who my friend really was, I wanted to be sure that I paid him handsomely.
I didn't want anything to interfere with the progress I had made. Elvis had said he didn't care whom I told about his existence; however, I

intuitively felt that he would not continue to talk to me at all if a Parisian positively identified him.

"Of course," I responded, embarrassed that I had been in such a hurry to call Marcia that I had forgotten to pay him. Stripping off several francs, I left a generous tip. Still, no matter how ridiculous, the thought flashed through my mind that I was bribing this old Frenchman to keep silent about the identity of my new found friend.

"*Merci beaucoup,*" he said. The cigarette never moved as he spoke.

Chapter Five

My imagination had been ignited by my excitement, Paris, and all the old World War II French Resistance movies I had seen. I ran all the way back to the hotel. I couldn't wait to tell Marcia about the upcoming evening. I again had to knock on the gate to gain entrance, much to the chagrin of the night watchman. Again I felt compelled to explain to him my late arrival. However, the language barrier proved to be too great an obstacle. I decided to leave well enough alone and went straight to my room.

The clock sounded four a.m. I was astonished at how late it was. The time I had spent with Elvis simply flew. As I entered my room, I was hit by a feeling of exhaustion. I decided to wait until the next day to call home. I curled onto the bed without pulling back the covers or removing my clothes. The exhilarating time I had spent with Elvis had worn me out. I found myself falling into a deep sleep.

I began to have a very colorful and vivid dream. It was a bright and sunny day. I was in a small rowboat with a beautiful petite blonde who evidently was French. We were drifting along the

Seine. I had the most content feeling that I could remember since I had left my job a year ago to search for a man who supposedly had been dead for twenty.

I had been ridiculed, doubted, and second-guessed, and I imagined rightfully so. This dream probably was a vindication of the journey for my subconscious ego. We simply drifted down the river looking at the sights of Paris and watching the occasional white fluffy cloud float above.

I was awakened the next day by a loud knocking on the door of my room, or rather, a loud banging.

"Monsieur, monsieur...it is Bastille Day. Wake up, it is time to celebrate. You can sleep tomorrow. Today is a day of celebration!"

I had completely forgotten that this was a holiday in France. I imagined that my meeting that evening with Elvis would be a raucous affair. The French were known to celebrate wildly their day of independence. I could only imagine what the theater would be like tonight.

I answered the door. The guard continued his exhortation that I join in the revelry. Reluctantly, I assured him that I would join in the celebration at the theater that night. I knew the partying would last into the early morning hours, as was the French custom. I crawled back into bed.

I was awakened still later by even more joyful celebration. Fireworks were exploding everywhere. I decided to head on over to the theater where Elvis would be later that evening.

I walked back to the West Bank area where we had met the previous nights. A restaurant called the Gypsy was situated halfway between the hotel and the Elvis Review. It was only a few blocks from the bar where I had met him. I wanted to stop at the Gypsy and have a bite to eat before I joined the throngs at his show. The restaurant easily took up half the block. The sidewalk out front was covered with tables and chairs as was the French custom.

Young couples strolled by holding hands, enjoying the sights and sounds of the holiday. I ordered a small salad garnished with truffles. My French wasn't very good. The waiter obviously was not impressed with my attempt to speak in his native tongue.

He returned with my order promptly, informing me in English that he would return with the bill as soon as I was finished. No matter what anyone says, French food is superior to any in the world. My meal was delicious.

As evening approached, the crowds walking past the Gypsy became more rowdy. I'm positive their wine intake had something to do with that.

It was hard for me to imagine that Elvis Presley lived in a city of this size and still had not been recognized. His idea of performing as himself was brilliant. How better to hide himself than to mimic himself. Evidently it had worked, as he seemed confident that he would not be discovered. As the time for his show approached, I found myself becoming somewhat downcast. As is often the case, this journey, which had started out so exciting, had become somehow strangely subdued.

I paid my tab and reluctantly left a good tip. I joined the crowds of celebrating people out in the streets. The neon lights of this district were bright, but none were as bright as those of The Elvis Review.

Robert Mickey Maughon, M.D.

Hundreds of people lined the sidewalk pushing to get in. Men and women alike were dressed like Elvis Presley and sported long sideburns and jet black hair. Many wore the sequined outfits for which the entertainer was noted. Some had guitars.

How was I going to get in? I asked a young boy who looked no older than sixteen if he had been here before.

"Mais oui! He is the best Elvis impersonator in Paris," he replied in broken English.

"How do we get in?" I asked, still amazed at the bustling crowds.

"Watch me," he said and then began to push and surge forward through the horde of people. Before I knew it, we were inside the building. It was old but well-kept. We climbed a staircase that led to a balcony. I guessed that the theater would hold three thousand people.

It was a surreal scene, a Jean-Paul Sartre book come to life. Clusters of people were giving their own renditions of favorite Elvis songs from "Blue Hawaii" to "Love me Tender." Some were discussing their favorite Elvis movies or their favorite scenes from particular movies. An American couple squeezed into the seat next to me. I don't know why Americans can automatically recognize each other, but they can. They looked at me sheepishly before they spoke, probably because they were squeamish about the ridiculous sideburns they both wore.

"Hi, we're Albert and Phyllis from Portland, Oregon."

"Hi, I'm Robert St. John from Memphis."

"We hear this is the best show in Paris," the pleasant young lady began, attempting to speak above the noise of the crowd.

"I hear he looks like we would want Elvis to look like at his age!" her husband added.

Remembering what Elvis had told me, I decided to test his theory. Marcia didn't count. He didn't understand how much faith that woman had in me.

I turned to them nonchalantly. I crossed my arms across my chest and said in a brazen manner, "He is Elvis."

Their faces froze in unison. Then a small smirk of disbelief crossed their faces.

"Ha ha!" Albert, the somewhat rotund but jovial Oregonian, let out a huge guffaw. He hit me on the back several times, almost knocking the breath out of me. He began to elbow Phyllis.

"I get it. Sure, it's Elvis. Don't you get it, Phyllis, it's the Elvis Review." His laugh grew louder and seemed to trigger her laughter. By the time they were both laughing, I just smiled and nodded my head.

"Robert from Memphis is a riot!" Phyllis said, as they both continued to get a big kick out of my "joke."

Elvis had been right. No one would believe me. I was tempted to turn to Albert and inform him that the grave site at Graceland had been excavated and the casket found unoccupied, but I held my tongue.

Suddenly the bright stage lights cascaded out over the audience. That silenced almost everyone, even the couple beside me.

A drum roll sounded the familiar cadence to the advance of "C.C. Ryder." This triggered the loudest and longest standing ovation I believe I have ever heard. Dozens of spotlights began to twist and turn crazily in every direction. The scene reminded me of Elvis' 1968 comeback special beamed live to the mainland from Hawaii.

An overhead voice blared, "Ladies and gentlemen, would you please welcome the 'King of Rock 'n' Roll', Mr. Elvis Presley, to Paris."

I had been wrong. I had thought the previous ovation was the loudest I had ever heard. Impossible as it seemed, this one was even louder. I had to momentarily cover my ears. I looked around. Everyone in the audience as far as I could see was dressed like Elvis, everyone but me. They were all screaming at the top of their lungs and jumping in their seats or dancing. It was pandemonium! I was at first taken aback by their outpouring of affection and enthusiasm. Then I realized they were applauding for arguably the greatest entertainer the world had ever known. Even though they thought he was simply the greatest pseudo-Elvis possible, I knew they were applauding the real thing. It gave me an immense sense of satisfaction. Other than Marcia, everyone had thought I was crazy to leave my home in Memphis and my new profession to try to find him.

I found myself caught up in the huge surge of pure adrenaline that flooded the amphitheater. I added a mental note to the list of questions I wanted to ask him. "Why was he still performing?" I think I answered my own question, though, when I caught myself singing "C.C. Ryder" with everyone else and applauding wildly. Elvis whirled and turned on the stage like a twenty-five-year-old and threw a scarf at a young mademoiselle in the front row. I quit thinking about myself. I quit thinking about anything but this bundle of performing energy onstage. I joined the rollicking mass around me in celebrating this Elvis orgy.

What a rush! Entertainers say there is no other feeling in the world like live performance. Tonight for the first time in my life, I understood. I somehow felt very proud for this man. I had only met him a few hours earlier, and I had not yet probed into why he had done what he had done. The old images of the bloated Elvis were gone. In their place was a picture of this seemingly eternally young performer on stage. It was as if he had completely changed his whole life, which I imagined he had had to do to metamorphose into this current dynamo.

His energy level was a phenomenon to behold as he belted out "Viva Las Vegas."

The next song he performed was "Return to Sender," a personal favorite of mine. When he sang the refrain, "Return to sender, address unknown, no such person," the whole audience joined in and I had to cover my ears again because the noise was so deafening. Elvis kept the crowd roaring as he sang "Heart Break Hotel," "Ain't Nothing but a Hounddog," and "Jail House Rock."

Albert and Phyllis tried to tell me something but all I could do was watch their lips move. I couldn't hear a word they were saying. I threw my hands up in the air and then pointed to my ears trying to get them to realize that I couldn't hear them.

Elvis then quietened the audience with his hand. The girl singers behind him began to hum. The stage lights were dimmed and turned to a blue hue. Then Elvis began singing "Wise men say, only fools rush in, but I can't help falling in love with you."

The girls in the front row stopped screaming and started crying. He reignited them momentarily when he threw more scarves to them, but that was only temporary. The entire theater became deathly silent when he started singing, "And now, the end is near." Everyone was crying or sobbing when he ended with the last few words "and I did it......my way"!

The drum roll that always ended his rendition of this song was thunderous. For many reasons, this song had come to mean a lot to me personally. I tried to be discreet as I dabbed at the wetness of my own eyes.

I glanced over to see if Phyllis and Albert had seen me crying. Phyllis was patting the mascara that was streaking down her face. Albert was honking into a large paisley handkerchief. His sideburns had loosened and were flopping around the side of his face. The bags under his red rimmed eyes made him look like a beagle puppy that had been crying. He looked ridiculous. Thankfully, Albert and Phyllis had been too busy attending to themselves to pay any attention to me.

It seemed as if the whole roof would cave in when Elvis bowed on stage. The curtain calls were too numerous to count.

I waved good-bye to my new acquaintances from Oregon and began to pry my way to the backstage area. I don't know how exactly, but the stage guard seemed to recognize me and let me back. I thought backstage would be tumultuous, but it wasn't. It was strangely quiet and deserted. If not for the continued roar of the crowd out front I would not have guessed this was the dressing area of the world's greatest performer. Or, I guess in this case, the world's greatest imitator of the world's greatest performer.

Elvis almost knocked me over as he ran back for one last curtain call.

"Doc, you made it!" he exclaimed breathlessly. He shook my hand as if he truly was glad to see me.

"Come on back," he shouted, trying to be heard over the roar that was demanding another curtain call.

He pulled me by my shoulder to the back of the area and led me into a small, cluttered dressing area. When he closed the door behind us, it shut out most, but not all of the remaining noise.

"Wow," was all I could say. I felt exhausted. I couldn't imagine how he must have felt.

"Have you enjoyed yourself? Did you like the show?" Elvis always made sure that everyone else was comfortable and enjoying themselves. That part of his reputation was well deserved.

"Hey, how about you coming over to the house and we'll continue our conversation?" The sweat beamed from his forehead. I knew he had to be exhausted, but he seemed truly interested in me joining him.

"I'd love to!"

"Let me take one more curtain call, and we'll slip out the back." He disappeared and returned to a thunderous ovation. After being gone for only a minute or two he returned. The PA's voice boomed behind him, cautioning everyone to be careful and to have a pleasant evening.

"Let me clean up some and we'll go."

Elvis disappeared behind a partition that evidently masked a shower and restroom. I took time to observe his small dressing room. There was none of the memorabilia that is usually associated with a major star. I imagine that was by design. There was one small picture of Elvis with an Elvis impersonator. It struck me as odd. Why would he have this? Was it a smoke screen? What still struck me as most unusual was that nobody else seemed to recognize him. The more I was with him the more I was sure that he was Elvis. It had been the hands at first. But now it was everything about him. His actions, the way he performed, everything.

I guess it was the power of the mass media that kept his identity safe. Since 1977, everyone had said he was dead: everyone except an occasional nut who claimed to have seen him at Kmart. Now I had a different opinion of those people, and *The National Enquirer* for that matter. I would have doubted my own sanity except I was absolutely, positively sure it was him!

"I'm ready," he called out as he emerged from the partition. "Come on." He pulled me past the guard and led me to a small door that I had not noticed previously. We found ourselves stumbling down a small hall.

"This will lead to the back alley. We can slip off down a side street. Home is just around the corner. I want you to meet my girl."

We entered the night air. He had picked up a light jacket on the rack just outside the stage door and slipped it on.

The side street we stepped onto was not busy at all. We could see the front of the theater and the main street. Hundreds were still milling about. Giant fireworks burst into air. The carnival-like atmosphere was contagious. We slipped down the narrow alley and headed for what he told me was a garden apartment next to the theater. We basically had not walked more than a few feet when we opened another small door in the alley and entered his home.

He fumbled around and flipped on a light switch, and a dim light came on. Elvis' home was a nice apartment surrounding a garden. It had none of the trappings of Graceland, but was in fact plain and subdued.

"Elvis, is that you?" a heavily French-accented voice appeared to come out of the dark somewhere. Suddenly the figure of the petite young French girl who had been with me in my dream last night appeared. I was astounded.

"Babette," he laughed as he went up and hugged the lovely young girl.

This was too unreal. First I was talking to Elvis Presley. Now people from my dreams were popping up into real life. This was too much. I tried to hide my surprise but apparently wasn't able to.

"What's wrong?" he asked, noticing the look on my face.

"Nothing," I said, trying to recover some.

"Glad to meet you, Babette," I said as I shook her hand.

She said something in French and then said, "How do you do, Monsieur Doctor Robert. My Elvis has told me about you."

It was apparent that for all the changes he had gone through, Elvis still loved beautiful women.

Chapter Six

I looked at him. He looked back with a noncommittal expression on his face.
Babette asked us politely but in a shy manner, "What would you boys like to drink?"
We both shrugged our shoulders. She said she was going to have a type of French champagne that I didn't recognize, and I said I would try it. She apparently knew what Elvis wanted because she left with a point of the finger as if to say, "I'll bring yours too."
"How do you like her?" he whispered as he motioned for me to have a seat next to him in the sitting room.
"She's beautiful," I proclaimed.
He smiled. "She reminds me of the way Priscilla was when she was that age. Not so much the way she looks but the way she acts. I like her a lot, but no one will ever replace Priscilla." His voice turned sad for a moment, then he looked up and said, "What did you want to talk about tonight? We were at the point where you had taken the medical examiner's job in Memphis when we finished talking last night."
"That's right. And I had just met Marcia."
"Tell me more about her, okay?"

"Sure. But first, let me ask you, does Babette understand English?"

"Only a little bit, or so she says."

"Does she know who you really are?"

"No, she knows me as the entertainer you saw tonight."

"So is this the way you make a living?"

"Yes," he nodded affirmatively. "Remember that the estate is controlled by Priscilla. That's not my money anymore." He caught himself after the last statement, holding up his hand. "Wait, we're forgetting our agreement. You're supposed to tell me how you found me, remember, and after your story, if I want to, I'll tell you mine."

Babette burst back into the room with the drinks. His mood lifted immediately.

"Merci beaucoup," he thanked her.

"You are welcome, Elvis," she struggled in her thick French accent. The small beauty then handed me my drink and curled up in his lap. Whatever hold he had over women certainly hadn't waned over the years. It obviously translated into French as well.

"Tell me more," he demanded. He sipped lightly from his glass. On both of the previous nights I had noticed that he really didn't drink alcohol. Perhaps tonight was special.

"I was at the point of taking the job."

"That's right," he said as he kissed Babette affectionately on top of her head. I took a sip of my drink, trying to remember where I had discontinued my story.

"I remember. I was at the emergency room. I had just met Marcia. She was seeing a little girl with an earache."

Elvis nodded.

The dark areas of the room lulled me into a calm state of mind. Babette curled up even more into his arms. I faded into the past as I recalled that day back in Memphis.

"I don't know why but we weren't able to go out that night. Maybe Marcia stood me up...I don't recall. It was a week...maybe even two weeks later that we finally had our first date. She was in a bad mood. Marcia had had a bad day in the emergency room. She bit my head off most of the night, but we moved in together within the month. I had never been around the dirty work that a medical examiner is exposed to that much. Autopsy work is gruesome at times. Thank God I had Dr. Bickley Cross and Marcia to help me those first six months.

"I was exposed to the most nauseating case in about the second or third month on the job. A small child had been abused then murdered, and when the body was discovered, it was badly decomposed. If I hadn't had Marcia, I might have quit right then and there. After all, there wasn't anything in Memphis to make me stay. My sister was six hours away in Knoxville.

"Yes, that case tore me up. It was right after that case that I was called back into Dr. Regent's office. I guess that's when I first began the long journey to find you." I pointed to Elvis.

"What happened?" he asked, having to peek above Babette's head.

Somehow, the way she held onto him made her appear more like his daughter than his lover. It reminded me that Priscilla had once told Barbara Walters that Elvis was many things to her, father figure included. Anyway, I began to explain how things unfolded one year ago in Memphis that led me to him.

* * * * *

"Dr. Regent called for you, Robert, while you were out," Marcia said when I returned to the hospital from inspecting the scene where the baby had been killed.

"What did he want?" I was still disgusted by the day's events.

"I don't know. He asked that I tell you to come by when I saw you."

I kissed Marcia. She had on her white coat with the medical name tag and ID that enabled her to get into the ER at the downtown hospital. I looked at my watch and decided I had enough time to go by and see him.

I liked Dr. Regent. He was a gregarious man. He always had a story to tell or there was someone of interest in his office. Mrs. Mason, the secretary who had taken me to see my apartment that first day, stopped me when I tried to walk right into his office. This was unusual as she usually let me in anytime.

She leaned over the table and whispered, "The governor's here to see Dr. Regent."

"The governor!" I whispered back in surprise. "What does he want?"

She leaned forward again, "It's something really hot politically, Dr. St. John. It involves the medical units…or something." She tried to appear in the know, but aloof and above the gossip.

"Well," I whispered back. "He called Marcia and said it was imperative that I come and see him."

"Oh." That threw Mrs. Mason a bit. She

hesitated before she buzzed Dr. Regent.

"Dr. Regent?"

"What, Mrs. Mason?"

"Dr. St. John is here. Do you want to see him this afternoon?"

"Good heavens, woman! Absolutely. Send him right in."

I looked at Mrs. Mason as if I knew I was very important and puffed out my chest.

Mrs. Mason didn't go for any of it.

"Okay, Dr. St. John. Dr. Regent and the governor will see you now." Her tone of voice let me know that she wasn't the least bit impressed with me, but she did so in the teasing sort of way that typified her personality. This attitude was why I had grown to like her so much. I exaggerated a salute at her "You may enter now" pronouncement and walked into Dr. Regent's office.

*****

"What did he want?" Elvis asked. He had leaned forward in his chair, holding the now asleep Babette with both hands.

I pointed at Babette and made a *shhh* sound.

He looked down at her and smiled.

"Let me put her to bed and I'll be down in just a second. Get yourself another drink if you want. It's over there in the fridge." He motioned to the refrigerator next to the wall in the corner. He scooped the sleeping Babette up in his arms and carried her across the room.

There in the darkness was a staircase that I had not been able to see. He deftly began to take her to what I assumed was an upstairs bedroom.

The lone light that was stationed behind the chair where he was sitting had blinded me to my surroundings. Now I was able to survey the room more closely. I got up and stepped over to the refrigerator. When I opened the door, its interior illuminated a stack of pictures lying on top of the appliance. I tiptoed to get a better look. One was of Lisa Marie. Another was of Priscilla. The last one was of Elvis' late mother, Gladys.

I opened the bottle of champagne. Pouring a full glass, I took my time and looked around the room. It really was rather spartan. The furniture and bare brick wall reminded me of a French chateau. There was a quilted rug on the floor. I didn't recognize the pattern. I slowly walked back to my chair. I could hear Elvis and Babette laugh upstairs.

I tried to look into the bedroom upstairs, but I couldn't. I could see a small sliver of light that escaped from the space of the cracked door. In a moment I could hear Elvis start across the upstairs floor. The crack opened widely, flooding the stairway with light. He bounded down the stairs.

"Hey, do you want to go sit out in the garden?"

"Sure."

He led me out a side door into an open-air garden, not large, but nice. A high red brick wall surrounded the whole space. A cluster of white wicker furniture was arranged in the center of the garden. He motioned for me to follow him and take a seat. He sat in an oversized rocking chair, and I sat on a love seat across from him. The July night was actually comfortable.

"So what did the governor want?" he asked curiously.

I took a small sip of champagne. Because I knew some of my story might upset him, I was walking on eggshells. I wasn't sure if he knew anything about the events of a year ago in Memphis. I had just earned his trust, and I sure as hell didn't want to lose it now. However, I didn't know how to tap dance around the story. I decided to tell it in a straightforward manner and let the chips fall where they may.

"Elvis, it was about you."

He nodded his head a little as if to say, "I thought as much."

I took another sip of champagne and began.

* * * * *

"Come in, my boy!" Dr. Regent greeted me in his usual loud and exuberant manner.

"Hello, Dr. Regent. How are you?"

Dr. Regent turned to Rex Chambers, the governor of Tennessee.

"Dr. St. John, have you met the honorable governor of our state, Rex Chambers?"

I extended my hand to Governor Chambers and said, "It's my pleasure."

He shook my hand and began some kind of pat political introduction: something about how he was glad to meet me and how he admired the work we doctors did. His handshake was firm but strangely annoying for some reason. His hand was sweaty. Maybe that was it.

Rex Chambers was a people's politician, if that's not an oxymoron. He could kiss babies with the best of them. That he was in Memphis didn't surprise me. After all, the University of Tennessee's medical units were funded by the state.

* * * * *

I paused and looked Elvis in the eye. I had grown to like the man. Strangely, I hadn't thought I would when I began looking for him. Now that I had seen the human side of him, I absolutely did not want to offend him. He was too nice of a man for that. It was as if he read my mind.

"Don't worry, Dr. St. John, you're not going to offend me. I might know a lot of this stuff already anyway."

"Okay," I said and restarted the story.

* * * * *

Governor Chambers took me by the hand as if I were one of his subjects. For a second I felt like one of the trophies hanging on Dr. Regent's wall.

"Dr. St. James—" Governor Chambers began.

"It's Dr. St. John," I interrupted.

"Excuse me...Dr. St. John," He started again.

Dr. Regent leaned back in his chair behind his desk, making himself comfortable. He lit up a cigar and began to blow smoke everywhere.

"I'm here because I'm a firm believer in covering all the bases," the governor continued.

"I don't believe anything will come of this, and I must interject that you must swear to secrecy everything that you hear in this room." The governor looked over to Dr. Regent for support. Somewhere in that cloud of blue smoke I could see the top of Dr. Regent's head bobbing up and down in agreement.

"Dr. St. John, I believe in covering my backside," the governor continued.

Dr. Regent leaned forward through the smoke. "Good Lord, Rex, get to the point!"

Rex Chambers harumphed a bit, adjusted himself and looked me straight in the eye.

"I'm here to forewarn you in case...in case this travesty comes to pass. Priscilla Presley called me several weeks ago and told me a shocking story. DELTA Records and their affiliated insurance company have threatened to file suit in Nashville to halt and actually ask for the return of royalties from the Presley estate." The governor began to pace back and forth in front of Dr. Regent and me.

"Those fools!" He continued. "They get into financial trouble and try a stunt like this!"

I looked at Rex Chambers and then to Dr. Regent and asked, "What does this have to do with me?"

"Listen to the governor, Robert. This is the damnedest piece of crap you've ever heard."

That caught my attention. Dr. Regent never cursed unless he was extremely upset.

"Winston Doyle, the CEO of DELTA Records, has threatened—no, promised—to have the remains of Elvis Presley disinterred!"

* * * * *

I looked over my glass of champagne at Elvis. He didn't blink an eye. He looked at me coldly. "Go on," was all he said.

I continued, still trying to gauge his reaction.

* * * * *

I sat in Dr. Regent's office dumbfounded. The

Elvis Is Alive

governor of the State of Tennessee was ranting like some lunatic. My boss, Dr. Regent, was sitting there in his own cloud of smoke, evidently agreeing with what Chambers was saying.

"How can they do that?" I asked. "That's preposterous! And beyond that, why would they do such a thing?"

The governor stopped in his tracks and looked me directly in the eye.

"Money!"

I must have looked like an idiot or something because he began to pace the floor again and said, "It's a well-known fact that the company that has paid millions of dollars in royalties to the Presley estate has been run to ruin by this arrogant fool, Winston Doyle. Now he's trying to save the company by abusing the law."

"What do you mean?"

"He's found a way, legally, mind you, to have Elvis' grave dug up and his casket opened."

I couldn't believe my ears. I was completely dumbfounded. "Why on earth would he want to do that?"

"Doctor, as I just said, money. Winston and his lawyers have come up with a way to stop royalty payments...even demand a return of all monies paid if the cause of death was suicide."

I looked at Dr. Regent. He looked at me with an expression that said "just listen."

"Do you remember a couple of years ago when there was an inquiry here concerning the exact cause of Elvis' death?" Chambers continued.

"Yes...I do. I wasn't in Tennessee then, but I remember."

"An obscure Tennessee law that Doyle and his

cronies have uncovered allows them to dig up the body and do another autopsy. If they can prove drugs were involved, then suicide could be inferred. A huge life insurance payout could be recalled, as well as having royalties stopped, at least temporarily."

I was beginning to get the story. If this crazy scenario actually played out, as the medical examiner, I would be on the hot seat.

"So let me get this straight," I began. "If these bozos can actually do this thing, I'm it."

Dr. Regent peered through the smoke again.

"That's right, Robert. If the Elvis Presley grave site is exhumed, by state law, the person who has be there under these circumstances is you!"

I tried to get up, but my legs were too rubbery.

"That's not all," Rex began, "do you know who Winston Doyle is whispered to be linked to?"

"No, I don't know," I replied, "but from the tone of your voice, I gather it's not good news."

"That's right, Doc. Underworld mob types."

Dr. Regent looked up from his desk. The color, or rather lack of it in his face, caught my attention.

"They're the type who would try to influence your findings, and not like it if you didn't find things their way," he warned. "Do you realize how much money we're dealing with here, Dr. St. John?"

"Millions?" I guessed.

"Many, many millions," Dr. Regent interrupted.

* * * * *

Elvis held up his hand for me to stop. I felt my heart sink. I had offended him and he would want me to leave.

"I have a beach house down near Marseilles. Would you care to join me and Babette for the next few days?" he asked.

"Yes," I said, as I accepted his invitation without hesitation.

Robert Mickey Maughon, M.D.

Chapter Seven

The French don't like McDonald's. They don't like Eurodisney. They basically don't like American culture, especially when it replaces anything French. They do, however, like trains. In America, we did away with trains when the automobile was invented. Not so in France. They never took to the automobile like we Americans did. They drive boxy little cars like the Peugeot. Of course, we do have trains in the U.S., but Amtrak doesn't count. You've got a fifty-fifty chance of reaching your destination on an American train. In France, they understand the superiority of a well-run train system. It's much more romantic in many ways.

We took a train to Elvis' beach-side home. The train was clean, fast and efficient. The food was superb. We in America love our automobiles, but I must admit the French have the right idea. Instead of spending money on big fancy cars, they put their money into a good train system.

Babette and Elvis must have honeymooned all the way to the beach. I didn't see them more than twice. On my own, I wandered throughout the cars. In the sitting car, I sat by myself and watched the countryside go by. It was beautiful. I tried to talk with a few French people but was rebuffed when they discovered how American my French was.

I had been away from Marcia now for several months, and I was lonely. I noticed three young French girls who were traveling alone. One in particular with dusty blonde hair was very attractive. I considered her a young Brigitte Bardot, especially after a few Jack Daniel's.

I thought of the lines of a song from my adolescence: *"Voulez-vous couchez avec moi ce soir?"* Will you go to bed with me tonight? I imagined myself approaching this comely young girl and whispering these words into her ear. After the Jack Daniel's had worn off, I was glad I hadn't. Elvis could have pulled it off, but not me. I would have messed it up and probably been slapped in the face. Besides, I wanted to remain faithful to Marcia.

Thinking about Jack Daniel's made me laugh. The French consume more wine than anyone in the world. They also produce the most. The Germans drink the most beer and probably produce the most also. And we Tennesseans make a damn good whiskey, Jack Daniel's. I could imagine the look of shock on French or German faces if I explained that in the county where this delightful concoction is made, you can't buy it. The South is a wonderful place, but it is full of contradictions and surprises.

The train made a beeline to Marseilles. The countryside was more beautiful than my native east Tennessee, if that's possible. It was definitely different, consisting of tiny communities of small farms surrounded by old stone fences that probably dated back centuries.

At Marseilles, we headed west toward the municipality of Monaco. The mere thought of that place brought flashes of kings and queens.

At the coast, the train stopped at a small station. It was four a.m. and still so dark that it was almost impossible to see. A small white sedan was waiting for us there. A slight, goateed older man wearing a burgundy beret stood ready to greet us.

"Pierre, how are you?" Elvis ran over and hugged the man.

His English was broken and uncertain, but Pierre seemed to be able to communicate anything he wanted. We had only a few bags, but the small car was crowded with the four of us and the baggage. Pierre and I sat in the front, Elvis and Babette in the back.

"I bought this home several years ago," Elvis said. "It's on the beach and secluded. It's also close enough to Monaco to enjoy some night life. I've entertained there some."

Hedgerows obscured most of the countryside. Darkness made the rest of it almost impossible to see. We drove down a small country road. It was asphalt but didn't seem to be much larger than a path. Pierre was speaking in French about some things that had been done around the house. It had evidently needed to be painted and was in the process of being spruced up.

The headlights of the car beamed onto a side path, which we took. It was obvious that we were very close to the beach. Sand dunes lined each side of the path. The house loomed ahead. It wasn't huge, but it was a nice beach home, completely Mediterranean in style.

The sun had begun to rise over the east. Pierre

Elvis Is Alive

pulled the car into the garage adjacent to the house.

"Come on in, Robert," Elvis said. "Pierre will bring in the bags."

We walked into the house. The first floor was spacious, opening out to the beach and the Mediterranean.

"Are you guys hungry?" Elvis asked.

"Not me. I am a little tired, though. I didn't get to sleep much on the train."

"It's probably a good idea if we all get some sleep," Elvis began as he noticed Pierre struggling to bring the bags into the house.

"Go on upstairs, Dr. St. John. You can sleep in the first bedroom on the right."

I reached around Pierre and grabbed the small bag I had brought with me.

Elvis pointed to the middle of the room where the stairs were located. I made my apologies and headed upstairs.

"The bathroom is to the right, overlooking the beach," he called up as I was halfway upstairs.

I acknowledged him with a small wave of my hand and headed on to my room. All the furniture was covered with sheets, and the smell of fresh paint hung in the air. The room had been painted a beautiful green, the exact color of the sea outside. I opened the window and felt the breeze from the water before pulling the covers back from the bed. The sun was really beginning to peek up from the horizon as I snuggled in. I had found Elvis Presley and was his house guest at his beach home. How lucky could a man be?

The sun was beaming hard into my room when I awakened. I was disoriented at first until the sound of laughter from the beach made me realize where I was. Looking out the window, I spied Babette and Elvis frolicking on the beach. I decided to join them. I slipped on a swimsuit I had brought from the States and headed downstairs.

The kitchen was located at the side of the large living room we had entered early that morning. Pierre was busy working and cooking. He smiled at me and pointed through the front door to the couple. I waved back at him and headed out the door. The muggy air hit me strongly as I went through the sliding glass door and to the front veranda. Elvis and Babette had moved about two hundred yards down the beach. I heard their laughter and screams before I could see them. Glancing up and down the beach I saw we were completely alone. It was a beautiful scene as trees and shrubbery were bent inland from the wind and extended down to the beach's edge.

I walked down the concrete path that led to the beach. The warm sand felt good under my bare feet. I ran to them, eager to share their exuberance and enjoy their company.

Elvis waved at me as soon as he saw me. He motioned for me to join them. I approached and decided I would only visit with them a little as not to intrude on their fun.

"Hey, did you have a good nap?"

"Yes, I sure did. Thanks. How's the water?"

"Great." Elvis pulled Babette close to him. "I'm having to entertain this young lady, and it's wearing me out." He patted the top of her head.

"Listen, we're going to Monaco tomorrow," he continued. "We're going to have some fun. I don't have to go back to Paris until next week. We want you to go in with us. By the way, Babette has a cousin there who she thinks would enjoy your company."

"I'd like to go, sure...but maybe I need to go solo." I began to explain.

"Oh come on, Dr. St. John, don't be a stick in the mud. You don't have to marry the girl. You're not married, are you?"

"No, I'm not married."

"Good, it's settled. We'll hang around here today and go in tomorrow."

Babette smiled and whispered lightly into his ear.

Elvis looked at me and said, "Babette said her cousin would like you."

I held up my hands in protest. "I'm involved with a girl back home. I'll go with the girl, but only as friends."

Elvis and Babette smiled at me.

"Sure, Dr. St. John, whatever you say," Elvis said. "It's your life. I'm just glad you want to go. Listen," he looked at me with a serious look, "the conversation we've been having..."

I jumped forward, instinctively feeling I must have imposed on him.

"Elvis, we never have to talk about that again," I said. "You've been more than nice."

He interrupted me. "Doc, I want to talk to you more about all that went on. I must admit I'm curious. It's just I have to go slow with it. I hope you understand."

"Absolutely! You've been more than gracious as a host."

Elvis' mood lifted. "Say, don't you want to know your date's name?"

"What?" I replied.

"Brigitte!" Babette laughed, holding onto Elvis' arm.

I shook my head and contorted my face in mock surprise. "Brigitte? Like Bardot?"

"Oui," Babette replied.

I must admit I liked that name. My curiosity was piqued. Then, suddenly I remembered Marcia back home. My enthusiasm waned a bit. Still, it wouldn't be wrong to go with them if things stayed on a friendly basis.

"Hey, do you mind if I make a phone call to my girl back home," I asked.

"No, just tell Pierre back at the house. He'll get you through to the States."

I walked back to kitchen where Pierre was humming a peppy little ditty. He was still busy preparing the meal.

"Pierre?" I waited for him to answer me.

He turned and asked something slowly in French.

I held up my hand to my ear and pretended to dial a telephone.

"Oh, *mais oui.*" He picked up a towel and dried his hands. Pierre then led me out to a small cubicle out next to the garage. He pointed to the phone. I nodded my head and muttered *"Merci."*

Pierre smiled and shuffled back to the kitchen. He was much more accommodating about my poor French than the majority of waiters in Paris. I still had to contact an operator in this part of France to connect me to the U.S. Fortunately, she spoke nearly flawless English and actually knew where Memphis, Tennessee was. She graciously connected me to the U.S. operator, who helped me contact the 901 area.

The phone rang several times, then the answering machine picked up my call. Damn, I wanted to talk to Marcia.

"Hello," Marcia's voice burst through the answering machine's ending beep.

"Marcia, how are you!"

"Robert, I thought you'd call me before now. I was worried."

"I know, Marcia. It's been an interesting trip. I'm with Elvis at his beach house near Marseilles, France."

I peeked over at Pierre. I didn't want him to listen to everything I said. It wasn't as if I had a big secret to keep from the old housekeeper, but I preferred that he not overhear my conversation.

"Marcia, this is great. I really like the guy."

"Has he told you everything about what..."

"No," I interrupted. "I'm not that far along yet. I've made progress, but I still haven't gotten him to agree to tell me everything. The agreement is that I tell him everything about myself and then he'll tell me about what made him do this...maybe. You know what's most difficult? Telling him how I got here, since nearly all the story revolves around that crazy stuff that concerned him in Memphis."

"I hadn't thought about that," Marcia said sympathetically.

"Every time I get to a new episode that seems to be painful to him, I stop there."

"Have you brought up the money?"

"No, I haven't gotten to that, but I think it's a lost cause. Besides, you know that's no longer the reason I wanted to find him."

"I know, I just thought I'd ask."

"You know what else? My idea of writing a book about all of this has also taken a back seat."

"Really?"

"Yeah, he's such a nice guy and people have been such jerks to him and his family. I'm going to do whatever he wants me to do. He's taken me in as a friend, and I could never betray his trust now."

"I guess it's been worth all the effort then, huh?"

"Yeah…yeah…I must say it has."

"Do you want me to rub all the naysayers' noses in the mud for you?"

"No, that's not necessary. I've been vindicated, at least in my own mind, and of course, I hope you still have faith in me."

"Of course, silly."

"After all that crazy stuff in Memphis, I hoped you did."

"Shoot, you had to find out."

"You know what else? I'm not sure that he's ever going to open up and tell me everything."

"Even after he knows how much you've been through to find him?"

"Yes, even after I tell him everything." I looked around again. Pierre didn't seem to be able to understand what I was saying.

"Do you want to come and see me?" I teased Marcia.

"I would if I could, but you know how it is…work and all."

"I know, I know, it's just that I miss you."

"Robert, I need to tell you something."

"What?"

"I don't know how to tell you this, so I'm just going to tell you."

A long silence followed.

"What, what is it, Marcia?"

"I've started dating other people." Her voice trembled.

I stood there holding the phone dumbfounded.

"Robert, I've missed you horribly. It's been so hard for me these past few months, you being gone and all. It's not like I'm going to marry the guy.... It's just that.... Well, Robert. It was you who didn't want to get married."

My head reeled and I got slightly dizzy. Marcia had stood behind me during the months when everyone else had laughed at me for undertaking this crazy journey. She had actually pushed me to try to find him. The reward money that Winston Doyle and DELTA Records had offered was her primary motivation at first, but I depended on her as an anchor to return to occasionally to remind myself that I was not insane. She had been the first woman I had cared about since the death of my wife, Betsy. I was hurt. But in reality, this was something I should have expected. She had wanted to get married. I didn't.

"I'm sorry, Robert. I still love you. But since you started on this quest, I've had to depend on myself. I didn't know if you were going to settle down ever again. This just happened. I didn't plan on it. I would have told you sooner, but I didn't want to upset you. I thought that now would be a good time, since you've found him."

"How long?" I asked, trying to keep my voice even.

"Robert, I've been seeing him for about two months. I felt I didn't have the right to tell you before. I know how you've depended on me to be your moral support."

"You're a free woman, Marcia." I said indignantly. "You wanted us to get married, and I didn't want to. This serves me right. Listen, I've got to go."

"Robert, please don't be mad at me. That's the last thing I want."

I attempted to appear unemotional and aloof, but I'm not sure that I pulled it off.

"Marcia, I'm not mad. I'd be lying if I didn't say I was disappointed. But I have to be realistic. You're a beautiful young woman. If I'd been smart, I would have married you. I really need to go now. Is it still okay if I call you occasionally?"

"Absolutely. Please do. And we'll talk about our whole relationship when you get back."

That was little consolation. I had taken this journey under the notion that it was something brave and noble. I knew many men who had lost their women because they messed around, played golf or drank. I was the first who had been dumped because of an obsession with a rock star.

Could I blame her? Hell, no. I meant what I said. She was young and beautiful. She was at her sexual peak. Marcia had stuck by me longer than most women would have. I had no one to blame but myself.

You damn fool, I criticized myself under my breath. You've accomplished your goal, but what a price to pay. I immediately felt deep remorse and humiliation. I recalled what so many of my colleagues had said. They called me a fool for leaving my career and refusing to marry a woman as talented and sweet as Marcia. I had been warned by a lot of people, but their pleadings had fallen on deaf ears. I thought I was in search of some type of Holy Grail. Sure, I had reached the vast majority of my goal. Even if I had known my quest would come between Marcia and me, I would still have pursued it, no matter what. I had lost her. Slowly, a great and pervasive resentment began to build in me. I walked past Pierre. The sitting room beckoned. The large glass window there gave me a complete view of the azure Mediterranean.

Here I was, five thousand miles from home. One year of my life was gone. For what? I had thought all along that I would find Elvis and be proclaimed a hero by his adoring fans. I'd be paid a huge ransom and return home to the woman I loved. Now that wasn't going to be possible. I began to seep deeper into the black emotional pit I was digging for myself. Self-pity began to exude from every pore of my body. How dare this man play this horrendous hoax on the world...and me. I hadn't even obtained a promise from him that he would explain everything to me. I had chosen this quixotic journey and now my life lay in ruins. I blamed him—Elvis.

The cheerful little song that Pierre hummed in the kitchen began to irritate me to no end. I wanted to scream, "Shut up!"

I walked back into the kitchen. I spotted a bottle of Jack Daniel's and poured myself a stiff drink. Pierre continued to hum. I took my sorrowful attitude and my drink and returned to my place in the sitting room. My mood spiraled downward. The thought of my beautiful Marcia in another man's arms made my hands shake in anger. Elvis Presley had caused all of this. I was going to let him know how I felt when he came back in the house. I took another slug of whiskey comfort. He could just pop up in a whole different country and attract a woman like Babette. Me, I had to work my ass off to find someone like her or Marcia. Elvis Presley…well he was Elvis, no matter where he lived. Not me. I had to prove myself. Sure, lots of women had told me I was attractive. But it's not every day one can find someone like Marcia, or, at least I couldn't. The resentment continued to well up in me and started to settle in my belly.

How ridiculous for this man, a man who had everything, to do what he had done. He left his career, family, and everything to go in search of another life. The whole thing was preposterous.

I caught my image in the mirror above the fireplace. I had gotten up to pour myself a second helping of Jack Daniel's. My reflection startled me. I stopped in my tracks and stared at the man staring back at me. I laughed so loudly that Pierre ran from the kitchen to see the cause of this outburst. I patted the old goateed chef on his arm and tried to reassure him in my best French that I was okay.

Was I actually blaming Elvis Presley for my demise? Absurd! I had no one to blame but myself. No one had made me go on this wild goose chase. Initially Marcia had begged me to stay with her. But no! I had to prove to everyone that I was right. My precious little ego had made me go skipping all over the world to prove my detractors wrong. I had to put them all in their place. I looked at myself long and hard. Elvis Presley might have been the spark that made me go on this journey, but it was my stubborn and stupid pride that had made me see it through.

I saw a man in the mirror that had done many of the things that Elvis had done. Left a family, career, the most important things in life—for what? His reasons were probably going to be a lot less selfish than mine. I laughed at the absurdity of my life over the past year. Marcia had stood behind me even though she had begged me to stop. However, I had insisted on proving myself. I wound up just like Elvis, with nothing. I sank back into the chair in front of the panoramic view of this, the most romantic body of water on God's planet, and felt like a fool.

The voices and laughter of Elvis and Babette brought me back to reality as they burst into the sitting room like two teenagers. Elvis' smile left him as he took one look at my long face.

"What's wrong, Dr. St. John?"

His voice was compassionate and comforting. Babette looked between him and me to try to understand what was wrong.

"I've lost Marcia." The shame I felt over that revelation and the emotion I was showing made me hang my head.

"I'm sorry," was all he said.

Babette whispered in his ear. He looked at me not knowing whether to speak or not.

Instinctively, Babette must have known something was wrong. French women are like that, or she understood English better than she had let on.

She fumbled around in her purse that was left in the sitting room and produced a picture. She pushed it under my nose and said, "Brigitte!" as she pointed to a gorgeous bikini-clad young woman. The swimsuit, if you could call it that, barely covered up her body.

I'm old enough to understand love, sort of. Marcia had put up with my absence as long as she could, and then she had chosen someone else. Fair enough.

I couldn't do anything about Marcia now. She was in Memphis. I was in France. Elvis Presley was my host. His girlfriend was going to introduce me to one of the best-looking young ladies I had ever seen. My mood began to spiral up.

Maybe I hadn't been such a fool in the first place. It's funny how life changes so suddenly sometimes. One minute you're feeling lower than low and the next you think you might just wind up on top of the world. In my experience, it's usually only beautiful women who can make such mood shifts possible. Bless their little hearts.

Elvis could see that I approved of the young woman presented to me. "You're going to like her, Dr. St. John. This photo really doesn't do her justice. She's better looking than that." He waved his hand at the photograph.

My eyebrows arched up. "Wow," I said, all resentment leaving me.

Babette reached up and whispered something else in Elvis' ear.

Elvis laughed out loud again.

"Babette says that Brigitte will like you because you're cute."

I immediately felt embarrassed about my feelings of just a few minutes ago. These people were so nice and seemed to really care about me. I didn't know what to say.

Pierre entered the room banging on a triangle to signal that lunch was ready. The emotions of the day had made me ravenous.

"Come on." Elvis pulled me on my elbow. "A man always feels better after he's eaten, especially after he's eaten one of Pierre's specialties."

His genuine friendliness made me feel guilty. No one had put a gun to my head this past year. It wasn't his fault that Marcia had fallen for someone else. The more I was around him, the more I understood how he had become the most popular entertainer the world had ever seen.

Chapter Eight

Pierre had set a beautiful table. Fresh-cut flowers were sprayed out above antique linen. There was an array of fresh breads and fruits. The colors made it look like a Van Gogh painting that was ready to dry. When we seated ourselves, I was amazed at how at home I felt. My hurt feelings of just a half an hour ago were gone.

Several courses were served. Chef Pierre obviously took great pride in his culinary ability. He smiled and laughed, especially when I asked for several extra helpings. The conversation was light and fun. It didn't matter that Pierre's and Babette's English was choppy. Somehow, all of the laughter allowed us to communicate.

The talk eventually turned to our trip to Monte Carlo. We decided that we would go to Monaco the next day. Elvis told us about his experiences entertaining in the great casino on a couple of occasions. I was impressed.

After we had completed our meals, we gravitated to the sitting room. The sun was gradually heading down below the horizon as we situated ourselves in the comfortable furniture. Babette sat on Elvis' lap on a small white couch. I chose a large, overstuffed, high-backed chair facing the sea.

Pierre brought in some kind of blueberry-flavored cognac.

He hurried about, making sure that each of our glasses were filled. It seemed that the cognac was special, having been distilled in a family or a private concern. Anyway, he seemed to take great pride in its zesty burst of flavor.

After Pierre had filled our glasses, he disappeared for a few minutes. Elvis and Babette told a funny story about how they had decided to move in together in Paris. One stumbling block had followed another. Elvis seemed to take delight in how silly everything had been. Babette snuggled up to him, laughing. They seemed very happy together.

Pierre returned with a guitar in his hand and requested some music, saying, "Please Monsieur Elvis."

Babette got up from her perch and began to jump up and down, begging Elvis to play. "Please Elvis, please."

He shyly took the guitar, looked at me and asked, "Any requests?"

"Yes," I said. "Sing something new!"

He seemed surprised. "You don't want to hear one of my oldies?"

"I have so many favorites, Elvis, it would be hard to choose. I thought you might have written something new."

"I have," he said as he began to tune the guitar.

Babette jumped up and down clapping her hands louder.

"Please Elvis, play the new one. The song you wrote about me."

"Okay," Elvis said as he began to tune and

strum the guitar.

"This is the song I wrote after I met Babette in Paris. I had just moved from Madrid, and I was very lonely. Then I met her." He motioned to the adoring girl next to him.

He didn't seem to notice the look of surprise on my face. This was the first time he had told me about himself before he had moved to Paris. I knew that he had lived in Madrid. He had lived there for sixteen months, to be exact. I had even found where he had lived and worked. This was the first thing in his past that was not common knowledge that he had told me about. Maybe it was a slip-up. I looked at him closely as he continued to tune the instrument. He didn't seem to regret having told me this private matter. Maybe he was eventually going to tell me everything about his reasons for disappearing from the kind of life most people would die for. I knew about most of his travels. I was dying to know why.

Would he tell me? I felt better about the situation now. Perhaps he would feel more comfortable with me as time went on. I wanted to know how he had gotten away with exposing himself and showing his vast talent to Babette and Pierre without telling them who he really was. Surely they weren't so blind. Surely, I wasn't the only person on this planet who recognized this most recognizable of men.

The implications of all of this was difficult to comprehend. Elvis Presley was about to play a new song for me. I realized how valuable this would be back in the States...hell, the world. I had made up my mind about one thing, though. I had lost Marcia due to this stupid quest. I was going to follow it through to the bitter end. I had only accomplished half of my mission. Now I wanted to get to know him and understand why he had done what he had done.

I had resolved that I would find him and bring him back into the limelight. The reward from DELTA Records had factored into the equation. That part of my plan had faded into the background as I had closed in on his trail. Being the only person who knew he was "alive" was a rush in itself. He had opened up to me a bit tonight and I was thrilled. I relaxed back in my chair and decided I would breathe in this personal performance from the "king of rock 'n' roll."

I hadn't noticed that famous sneer since I met him that first night in Paris. I had wondered if that was by design. He showed it now as he began to strum the guitar gently.

"Dr. St. John, I was a depressed dude when I met this young lady. I had been in Paris only a little while." He continued to stroke the instrument, bringing beautiful chords out, filling the room overlooking the Mediterranean.

He seemed so happy. His humming and playing the guitar renewed my visions of him playing in the U.S. I knew I was letting my enthusiasm get in the way of my reasoning and common sense, but the thought of presenting him again to his fans made adrenaline course through my body in waves.

He walked slowly around the room, looking alternately at me and Babette as he strummed the guitar and hummed.

"The name of this song is 'Paris Nights,'" he said. He continued to strum slowly and then started to sing. His jet black hair fell down across his face.

His Cherokee heritage and genetics had kept his skin taut, and it glistened slightly from the humidity. I continued to be amazed at how his presence was so overwhelming when he performed. The power of an entertainer of his caliber on the human spirit is phenomenal. I could feel my pulse quicken in anticipation. He looked at all of us and smiled.

He began to sing of his time in Paris, of how a woman had saved his spirit and soul.

One thing that had always struck me about Elvis was the deepness and richness of his voice. He made you feel the power of what he was singing. When he hit the refrain, "Blue Paris nights/Dark Paris nights/Loneliest nights of my soul/Darkness took me to the deepest low/Till she opened sunshine's door," I felt chill bumps crawl over my back and settle on top of my head and into my scalp. It wasn't the words of the song that were brilliant; it was his presentation. When Elvis sang, God came down and blessed us mortals with a glimpse of what eternity could be: all power, richness and goodness.

This song was sung from the depths of his heart. He felt these words. He had lived these words. He had that rare ability to make you live and feel them too, even if just for a moment.

I had always been told that Elvis wasn't that smart. Bullshit! Any human who could write and translate human emotion through a performance like the one he was giving now transcended intelligence. Maybe he wasn't book smart, but he was a genius. Very few human beings had ever tasted from the cup that he was lustily drinking from now.

He was able, with a few simple phrases and an unbelievable voice and a beautiful persona, to describe the loneliest feeling imaginable. And he was also able to translate those feelings to his audience with a simple performance. It would have taken Hemingway an entire novel to explore it, to explain it. And Ernest was one of God's chosen few also.

Elvis Presley did it with one five-minute song. He may not have been considered to have been a brilliant man by those who supposedly knew what that meant, but to his great legions of fans around the world, he had been smart beyond measurement. Even the least intelligent among them had seen his genius for what it was, a glimpse into heaven. Elvis was a common man, just like them. He had been touched with a gift from God, and now I was a witness to that genius. I was in awe.

When he finished, Babette, the inspiration of the ballad, ran up and clasped her arms around his neck. Big tears streaked down her face, leaving winding paths in her make-up. She kissed him repeatedly on the cheek and the lips. She spoke excitedly in a hushed tone,

"I love you, Elvis. I love you."

Pierre clapped wildly. His goatee bobbed up and down. Pierre forgot the age his body had become. He stood up shakily on his chair and stomped his foot. It would have been comical if he had not been sincere and I had not been a witness to the powerful performance that had precipitated his adulation.

Elvis smiled. He bowed slightly, taking Babette lower with him, obviously surprised by the outburst.

I caught myself clapping so hard that my hands hurt. He had made me forget the loss I had felt earlier that evening. I was a witness to why he had been so popular, even after his death...or rather, disappearance. No wonder he had been spotted all over the world. Elvis was alive. My five senses told me that. He stood for the great things that a human being could be. Those things would never die, could never die.

People could not let him die because that would have been an admission of the mortal nature of all human beings. It's the nature of all of us to deny mortality. Elvis was a symbol of immortality. A symbol that powerful could not be easily taken away.

After my stinging hands would allow me to clap no longer, they found themselves wiping tears from my face. Why was I crying? I don't know. I had cried slightly the first night I had met him. Why? Search me. I wish there was some big, deep meaning to this emotion that I felt. Curiously, I didn't question it that much.

I took these tears as perhaps a vindication of the time and things I had lost in my search for him. I had witnessed him elicit such strong emotion in others before me that I didn't question this feeling. Nor was I ashamed of its manifestation. Strangely, it felt normal. All I could think of was how blessed I was at this particular moment and place in time. How differently I felt now than I had just a few hours earlier.

It took just one song to do it. A song sung by a very special man. I had become much more knowledgeable and understanding of the power he had over his admirers. Often, I had been a little

Elvis Is Alive

suspicious of their blind loyalty. Now I understood. Somehow, it made me feel closer to my maker, and I was glad that it did. For the first time in my life, I was not ashamed of the emotional nature of being a human being. I had finally understood that emotion is one of the most precious aspects of being human.

Pierre got off his chair. Babette moved away from him. I simply stood there.

"Thank you very much!" His humble thanks were appealing. "Do you want to hear anything else?" Elvis asked.

It wasn't that we didn't care to hear more, but the song had been a perfect ending to a lovely evening. Pierre said he would get more drinks. Babette walked back up to Elvis, putting her arm around his waist.

I walked over to the picture window. The Mediterranean was now covered with a soft darkness. Only the cast of pale yellow moonlight lit up the area. Everything seemed wonderful.

I had lost a lot. Marcia. My career probably. But I knew now that I had not made a mistake. Would I trade all the prestige a medical career can bring for the precious moments I had just experienced? No, I honestly wouldn't.

The sound of the surf in front of me was comforting. I thought of the trip to Monte Carlo with anticipation. I looked forward to meeting Brigitte, but most of all, I wanted to spend more time with this remarkable man. He made me feel like your parents do when you're a child and they tuck you into bed...comfortable and without a worry in the world.

Pierre returned with another glass of cognac. I

took a deep drink of the liquor, imagining that I was taking a deep drink of life. Maybe I was. Anyway, the feeling of the night was infectious. I looked back at Elvis. He held up his glass in salute.

"Let's toast my new friend, Dr. Robert St. John."

Babette toasted me also.

"*Monsieur* Doctor St. John."

She turned to Elvis, "A friend of Elvis." Her deep French accent made it difficult to understand, but I appreciated her sincerity.

Babette and Pierre held up their glasses again. I felt my face turning pink, but I had enough presence of mind to hold up my glass in return and say, "Hear, hear."

We all took a deep drink and laughed. I knew in my heart that I should be offering a toast to him, but his gesture made me feel special.

Babette was tugging at him, looking intent on getting him alone upstairs. It seemed that the music had ignited the passion she felt for him, or so I surmised. Maybe it was late and she was just tired. It makes a more romantic story to believe the former reason. He whispered something past her blonde hair into her ear.

Her face brightened and she said something that sounded like "okay" in her heavy English. She then began to excuse herself from the small gathering. In the dim light, I couldn't help but notice how attractive she was. She hurried up the stairs, stopping at the third step to blow Elvis a kiss, then disappeared.

"You have quite a young lady there," I said admiringly.

"I know," was all he said.

Pierre said something in French. Elvis

responded. He obviously considered Pierre to be more than a caretaker. From what I understood, that's the way he had treated all of his employees.

Pierre saluted us and went back into the kitchen. I could hear him walking around, cleaning and washing the utensils from the evening meal. I could hear him lightly whistling the melody from "Paris Nights." Even though Elvis had performed the song in English, Pierre had understood it and obviously liked it. Elvis picked up the guitar and placed it gingerly on the couch.

"Hey, let's go outside and get some air. The night air off the Mediterranean is phenomenal this time of year." He politely slid open the glass door and allowed me to walk through in front of him.

If I had a hundred things I wanted to ask him before tonight, now I had at least a million. I bit my tongue though. It wouldn't be polite. That was the Southerner in me. Besides, I was still afraid of scaring him off. Earlier my story had bothered him enough to ask me to back off. I was going to respect that wish. I wasn't going to burden this man who had become my friend with my burning curiosity and the myriad of questions that my inquisitiveness had produced. No, I would allow him space. In due time, if he opened up to me, that would be great. If not, that had become okay by me too.

Chapter Nine

"Did you like my song?" He broke the still silence of the night. Only the sound of the waves splashing on the shore competed with his voice.

"Like it? I loved it!" The enthusiasm in my voice surprised me.

He smiled and nodded his head in grateful acknowledgment.

"Dr. St. John," he began to explain, "I want to hear the rest of your story. I really do."

"Hey, you don't have to explain anything to me," I offered in understanding.

He held up his hand for me to hold on.

"It's just that it's obvious that some of what you're going to tell me has the potential to really upset me, and as you can see, I have a rich and full life here. I may not be ready to hear all of it. I want to think it over, okay?"

"Yes, I understand. I feel honored that you've allowed me to get this close to you. I'm a lot more grateful than you will ever know." I hesitated.

"What?" he finally spoke up.

I still was reluctant.

"Go ahead, Doc. If it's something that I don't want to answer, I won't."

Elvis Is Alive

I couldn't contain myself anymore. "It makes me feel like I'm crazy. I know who you are. It's so obvious to me that I can't believe that no one else has suspected it. Doesn't anyone ever come up to you and say, 'I know it's really you, Elvis!'"

He shrugged his shoulders and looked out over the water. The moonlight lit up his unlined face.

"It's like I told you before. I have a perfect disguise if someone insists that it's me." He said again, nonchalantly. "Have you ever counted the number of Elvis Presley impersonators?" He held up his right index finger in the air in a moment of illumination. "No, I tell you what, Dr. St. John. The better question is, have you seen some of them?"

The puzzlement must have shown on my face. "Yeah," I stumbled around, trying to catch his meaning. "Most of them suck!"

He laughed out loud in that big laugh that I had come to appreciate.

"Yes, yes...I guess maybe that's true. But," he held up his other index finger in protest, "there are enough of the Elvis impersonators out there who are good enough to muddy the water. It works! Listen, I'll tell you a secret. That's what I've told Babette."

I looked over at him in disbelief. "Oh baloney. I don't believe you."

"I was taught never to lie by my Mama, and I sometimes don't feel comfortable with this whole charade, but what else can I say? It's the life I've chosen. I'm able to do everything I want to do being an Elvis impersonator."

The sheer absurdity of that statement caught us by surprise. We both laughed.

"Enough questions tonight, Dr. St. John. Let's enjoy the evening. We have a big day ahead of us tomorrow. Let's enjoy it all. Have you ever been to Monte Carlo?"

"No, I never have," I answered, knowing I had pushed the conversation as far as it needed to go.

"You'll love it! It's one of the most beautiful cities in the world, if you ask me. It's very romantic."

His exuberance was contagious. I could hardly wait to go. It was another leg in my remarkable journey.

Elvis and I spent the rest of the evening talking about lots of little things. Most people would call it small talk. He asked me a lot of things about Memphis and about my family. He seemed to have a genuine interest in me and my career. Whenever I reverted back to my curious self and asked a probing but innocently posed question about him, he gently directed the conversation back to other subjects. Soon we both tired. Since we had a trip to look forward to the next day, we decided it was best to go to bed before the sun came up. We made sure the lights were off and headed to our respective bedrooms. I felt like I had just gotten comfortable in bed when the sun brightened the room, awakening me.

I got up to shower and could barely hear voices from downstairs. I hurried as not to miss anything. In my excitement, I actually ran downstairs to join them.

"Good morning," I announced, as I skipped down the steps.

Everyone looked up from the table and waved. Babette was seated close to Elvis. Pierre attempted to ask me in English if I wanted breakfast. I shook my head.

"Coffee only, please," I said.

"Are you ready?" Elvis asked as he took his attention away from Babette momentarily. They appeared very much in love. I was happy for them.

"Yes, I'm really looking forward to it," I confessed.

"I've grown to enjoy visiting new places," Elvis said, "especially the exotic and special ones like Monte Carlo. Do you like to gamble?"

I shook my head. "I've never had that much of an opportunity. I've been to Vegas, and to the Crystal Palace in Nassau once. I played slot machines mostly."

I was somewhat embarrassed about my lack of worldly experience. I had never had much desire, or the time, to gamble. I thought my admission of having played the slots made me look like one of those old ladies in tennis shoes lugging around a bucket of quarters. Elvis, of course, had ruled Vegas for years.

He took a sip of coffee. Matter-of-factly, he noted that he didn't really like to gamble either.

"My mother told me not to. She said it could grab you like alcohol, but I do like to play 21. It's fun. The casino is noted for that, you know."

"Hey, I'd like to learn to play. Would you teach me?"

"Be glad to. You'll enjoy it."

We finished our coffee. Babette had a sweet confectionery item kind of like a croissant. She playfully tried to feed part of it to him.

"Eat, Elvis!" Babette demanded.

He patted his taut belly and protested that he had to watch his weight. She insisted and finally succeeded in getting him to eat a bite or two. Their playfulness made me a bit envious. I was eager to meet Brigitte. I was always one to look forward to meeting a pretty lady. Elvis and I had that in common.

Pierre would hear none of my protests and plopped a large breakfast down in front of me. I felt obligated to a least attempt to enjoy his meal, even though my appetite for breakfast has never been strong. I mostly pushed everything around on my plate, but I did make an attempt to appear pleased.

After numerous cups of coffee and a minimal amount of conversation, we decided that it was time to head to that tiny municipality, Monaco. I learned that Pierre would not be going with us. Although he and Elvis had not been together very long, he seemed to have a great deal of loyalty for his employer. Elvis seemed to trust him to take care of everything.

I was somewhat disappointed that he wouldn't be going. He was strangely reassuring. Older people are like that sometimes. They take everything in stride, never seeming to get upset. His little ovation on top of the chair the night before had endeared him to me. If the beach house had been mine, I would have wanted someone like Pierre to take care of it.

It was around ten o'clock by the time we had loaded up our things. I shook Pierre's hand goodbye. I think he understood how much I had enjoyed his hospitality. He patted me on the shoulder as I crawled into the back seat of the Peugeot. All of us waved wildly at Pierre as we drove out the front driveway. Slowly, he and the beautiful beach chalet disappeared in the background.

The small boxy car did not fit Elvis Presley's image. Seeing his face in the rearview mirror peering intently at the road almost made me laugh. I pictured him in a Jaguar or Ferrari, not a Peugeot, that most bourgeois of European automobiles. No matter the make of his car, Babette didn't seem to care. She clung closely to his side as he drove. I had come to appreciate her innocence, and I was happy she seemed so devoted to him. After having lost Marcia in such a hurtful manner, I was glad that my new friend had such an affectionate girl.

Since I had left a part of my life, these new friends made me feel like part of a whole new life. The sun was shining brightly that morning as we drove through a particularly beautiful part of France. The sunshine, the beautiful view, the company of my new friends and the image of the vivacious Brigitte awaiting me combined to boost my spirits skyward.

"There's a great hotel next to the casino where we'll stay. It's convenient and elegant. You'll enjoy it, Dr. St. John," Elvis grinned at me in the mirror. "Besides, Brigitte lives very close to it." His grin got bigger as he laughed a mischievous laugh.

Babette hit him on the shoulder and turned around and smiled at me.

She said, "Don't pay any attention to Elvis. You'll like Brigitte."

The road wound crazily through the hilly terrain. Babette's blonde, mid-length hair blew in the breeze from her open window.

We slowly wound our way toward the small burg that had become a playground to the world's rich and famous, the beautiful people. Monte Carlo is home to some of the world's most beautiful homes and elegant yachts. There, caviar and champagne are consumed in uncountable quantities. There's probably no better place in the world than Monte Carlo for a disheartened man to forget his woes.

We stopped at a small border station that contained the customs depot. The lone old border agent eyed us all suspiciously. He inspected each of our passports through his spectacles as if they were a magnifying glass. This road was so slightly traveled that we must have seemed to be special customers to him. Finally, he grunted approval and stamped our books. Of course, he had to wink at Babette before we pulled out of the old wooden station—after all, he was French.

The road seemed to wind even more afterward, almost defying the law of nature. Finally, we crossed over the summit that had obscured the awaited city and the encircling Mediterranean from view.

"God, it's beautiful," I said, understanding at once why all the rich people party there. Huge yachts with swimming pools and helicopters lined the bay.

As we circled down from the mountain above, I was struck by how the whole city seemed white, especially in the bright sunshine. Babette snuggled even closer to Elvis as we all surveyed the magnificent view unfolding below us. I had thought Paris was beautiful, but somehow it seemed to pale next to Monaco's capital. We wound lower and lower, and the closer we got, the more romance seemed to wash up from the sea. Grace Kelly. Cary Grant. This was Hollywood without all the glitz. This was elegance with class. The feeling permeated every pore of my body the closer we got. I was going to do the town with Elvis Presley.

I saw very interesting architecture in the giant hillside villas as we drew closer to downtown. How they stayed perched on the steep terrain was beyond me.

"Look! There's the casino," Elvis said as he pointed at a large building near the center of town.

Many wonderful movies had been filmed at the casino. It had become a symbol for this tiny monarchy, that and the azure bay filled with yachts.

The traffic into Monte Carlo was minimal. We drove up to the Hotel Royale, which is close to the casino. The car was taken over by a tuxedoed youngster, and a tuxedoed bellhop who took us straight to our rooms. We didn't even have to check in.

"Room 525," the young man said as he stopped at a door. "Room 526," he said, looking at me, obviously giving me another room separate from Elvis and Babette.

"I hope its okay. I mean your room," Elvis said, slipping a heavy pair of black sunglasses down from the crown of his nose.

"Oh yeah...this will be perfect," I responded somewhat awkwardly. I hadn't expected to stay with them, but I hadn't been in on the arrangements. Pierre had taken care of all of that, so I didn't really know what to expect when we arrived. I hadn't felt like a third wheel on the way down here in the car, but now I did.

After the bellman had deposited my two bags at the appropriate place, I walked over to their room. I knocked lightly on the door, which was ajar. As I opened the door, I glanced past the bellman in order to get a glimpse of the opulent master suite.

It was obviously a special room. A large blue canopied bed took center stage. The bellman took a gratuity from Elvis and slid by me. Babette gleefully inspected every part of the room and its ornate furnishings.

"I feel that I'm intruding," I blurted out.

"Oh no, not at all," Elvis reassured me. "I was always used to having a lot of people around." He slid his sunglasses back up on his forehead. I was shocked at how much he looked like the Elvis of 1968, dark hair and sideburns. I still had occasions such as this when the realization that I had found Elvis and was actually talking to him simply astounded me. This was one of those times.

"What's wrong?" he asked, noticing my hesitancy.

"Nothing." I reclaimed my sense of reality. I reached out and shook his hand in gratitude and friendship.

"Babette and I wanted privacy, of course, but we wanted you to be next to us," Elvis said. "She is awfully fond of Brigitte," he said, motioning over at Babette.

"She wants you to stay close by so we all can have fun together." His sincerity made me feel better.

"Well, I insist on paying for my room. This has to be expensive." I had no way of knowing his financial status, although I did remember him saying that the Presley estate was no longer his. It would be rude of me to quiz him about the status of his current finances. I didn't want to be intrusive, physically or financially.

"Nonsense! Besides, this room is complimentary of the establishment."

"Complimentary?" I didn't understand what he meant.

"Yes, I've performed here before...as an Elvis impersonator," he explained. "They have a great tradition of entertainment here in Monte Carlo. The Casino really likes to take care of their favorite entertainers."

Good! Since he wasn't footing the bill, I felt less like an imposition.

"Come and look out the window." He pulled me enthusiastically to the balcony. We stepped outside onto the small balcony overlooking Monte Carlo. The strong breeze that greeted us was refreshing. I loved the weather spawned by the Mediterranean. This window allowed all of the freshness into the room. Looking to the right, we could glimpse the Casino. Directly in front of us were the docks with the huge yachts floating silently in the blue sea.

"Do you see that big yacht to the left?" He pointed to one in a line of boats.

"Which one?"

The Wandering Lady." He was pointing to the largest yacht I could see in the harbor.

"We're all going to go to a party there tonight after the casino."

"Who owns it?" I asked.

"A friend of mine who enjoys my impersonation act in Paris, Alfonso Buggatti, heir to the car fortune."

"Nice boat! Do you know everybody?"

"I like to think I do. If I don't, I hope I'll have the opportunity to meet them," he joked.

I think one reason Elvis is such a great entertainer is that he really enjoys people. It's something one can't fake, and he's been rewarded for this with a sincere loyalty that has been well documented. Of course, his ability to entertain has a great deal to do with his popularity as well.

"Brigitte! Brigitte!" Babette's shrieks grabbed our attention. We turned away from the balcony, and were greeted by the image of two cousins circling joyfully around the room, arms interlocked. They were obviously very fond of each other. Brigitte was sporting a large, floppy-brimmed hat that obscured her face.

Elvis and I stood motionless as the two continued to express their mutual affection. I leaned a little to my right. I wanted to get a better view of Brigitte's face. The hat afforded me precious little opportunity to glimpse her face as they continued to twirl in front of us.

The picture Babette had shown me had given me an excellent view of her physical stature, which was very impressive. The shadows that had highlighted the voluptuousness of her body had hidden her face. I was curious. Was she as pretty as Babette? It would help me get over the sting of losing Marcia if she was.

"Monsieur Doctor Robert." Babette stopped in the middle of the celebration, dragging Brigitte over to me. My heart skipped a few beats as I stood forward, preparing to meet my blind date.

"Beautiful." The word almost escaped from my lips.

She was pretty, very pretty. Her white smile seemed to illuminate her whole face. Brigitte took off her hat, shaking her mid-length auburn hair and letting it fall down to her shoulders. She was taller than her picture had revealed. And her green eyes were like dark, rich emeralds.

Elvis nudged me in the back, knocking me forward like a shy school boy. I would have nudged him back in retaliation except Brigitte had grabbed me by the face and planted two big kisses on either side.

Damn, my face turned red, so red that it burned. I wish I didn't do that, but there wasn't much I could do about it.

Elvis laughed a big laugh when he saw my surprise, which only heightened my embarrassment.

Brigitte turned to Babette and said something very rapidly and excitedly in French.

"She thinks you're cute," Elvis whispered to me as he nudged me again. This time he was standing close enough to me that I nudged him back with my left shoulder. It's funny how people never really grow up when it comes to the opposite sex. Elvis was close to sixty; I was forty-one. We were acting like a couple of teenagers in front of two girls, showing off in a way.

"Tell her I like her too," I managed to whisper, hoping Elvis would translate or that Babette would understand and tell her cousin.

Brigitte and Babette took turns at being silly in front of us now. They spoke in low tones and giggled, turning back and forth in front of us. Finally Babette looked at me and said, "Brigitte knows that you like her. She could tell by the way your eyes got big when you saw her."

I didn't turn red this time. A big smile crossed my face, then for some stupid reason I decided to say something in French. *"Bon soir"* popped out.

Robert Mickey Maughon, M.D.

Why I decided to say "Good night" I'll never know.

Brigitte and Babette clasped each other tightly and wheeled away from us, laughing uncontrollably. My face really got red then! I turned around to Elvis.

"What did I say that for?"

He grabbed me by the neck and pulled me to him.

"Hey, she likes you. They thought that was cute. You said something in French. That wasn't silly. Look at them." He turned my head over to where they were still laughing.

Brigitte gave me a flirty little wave and said, "*Bon soir*, to you, *monsieur.*"

"See, she likes you," Elvis said in a reassuring fashion.

Elvis clapped his hands together and said " Let's all go to the wharf and get some lunch."

"*Oui, oui,*" both girls agreed. Although they were in their late twenties or early thirties, their enthusiasm reminded me of high school cheerleaders. It was infectious.

"Hey, that's a great idea!" I concurred. "Let me clean up, and I'll be ready to go."

I started to walk out of the room. Turning back to Elvis, I asked, "What are you going to wear?"

"Slacks and shirt." Elvis made the okay symbol with his hand.

I walked past the girls, giving Brigitte a nod. Both girls smiled back.

I strode from the suite and hurried back to my adjacent room.

Somehow, this journey had turned out to be entirely different from what I had imagined. Perhaps I was building a new life for myself. I certainly was making new friends. My former life as a medical examiner in Memphis now seemed strangely unfamiliar.

I shaved and showered rapidly, in anticipation of a wonderful outing with Elvis, Babette and Brigitte. The hurtful feeling that had enveloped me after my last conversation with Marcia was gone. The year-long journey that I had endured was vindicated, not completely, but almost. The goal I had set for myself at the beginning now seemed ridiculous. I was still committed to finding the answer to my questions about Elvis' disappearance, but I was no longer interested in making them public. Monetary gain was no longer a consideration. If Elvis Aron Presley never wanted to explain why he had dropped from public view, that was okay with me. I was still curious, and I knew that I would ask him his reasons why if given the opportunity. But I wouldn't push or probe. He was my friend now, and I respected him.

The four of us walked out through the foyer of the grand old hotel into the bright Mediterranean sunshine. There was a fisherman's market and an outdoor seafood cafe at the far end of the bay. In actuality, very little fishing was done here. Most, if not all of the seafood was imported from various locations globally.

Babette and Elvis walked hand in hand in front of us up the cobblestone street fronting the sea. Brigitte and I attempted to talk but had a difficult time communicating. My French and her English seemed to mix like oil and water. Still, we had fun. When her petite hand clasped mine, there was no mistaking the communication that rushed between us. This was the universal language that needs no translation.

We followed the lazily strolling Elvis and Babette. After Brigitte and I began to hold hands, we became much more comfortable with each other. Funny, but our ability to communicate seemed to increase tenfold simply by holding hands.

We found ourselves at the end of the cobblestone walkway leading to the restaurant. Brigitte had made the walk seem very short.

We were seated promptly at the restaurant. La Pesca accommodates approximately seventy-five people, and it was crowded.

The waitress put us at a table that actually extended out over the Mediterranean. The ocean waves lapped against the floor beneath our feet. I felt alive again. My search of the past year had been so intense that I had begun to feel numb. I realized how lucky I had been that Marcia had stuck with me as long as she had. I wouldn't have put up with everything that she had. I found myself hoping she would find happiness. That bit of chivalry made me feel a lot better about myself. I wondered if I would be so generous with emotionally letting Marcia go if the beautiful Brigitte was not sitting next to me. Accidentally, her knee grazed mine and the image of Marcia and home faded.

"Dr. St. John, what are you going to have?" Elvis' voice rattled me a bit. I had been lost in thought and in Brigitte's green eyes.

"Shrimp.... That's what I like...shrimp," I stuttered.

Everyone began to eagerly pore over the menus that were provided at the tables. Brigitte and Babette leaned over the table, facing each other,

Elvis Is Alive

and talked excitedly. I assumed they were discussing the food they were going to order, or us.

The waitress came over to the table and began to discuss the catch of the day. She alternated between French and English. It's amazing how the French people always recognize Americans. I'm beginning to think a course in "recognizing the foreigners" is taught in the schools there.

Elvis ordered for Babette and himself. Brigitte ordered the catch of the day, squid, and I requested sauteed shrimp. The girls began to lean forward again and continued the discussion they had been engaged in before the waitress' interruption. Elvis finally got up and made Babette switch places with him so they could be side by side.

"Does this remind you of when you were a kid and dating?" he asked.

"Yeah, it does," I replied, adding, "I imagine that all girls do that." I motioned to Babette and Brigitte as they continued to talk excitedly.

"Why do girls always have to gossip and discuss their dates?" Elvis asked, leaning over close to me to preserve the confidentiality of his comment. "It must be some kind of universal rule or something."

Whack!

Babette's English must have been pretty good, as she playfully hit him over the head with her napkin in protest to his comment.

He ignored her.

"I remember when I was younger with... Priscilla...or whoever...the girls for some reason would always have to 'discuss' things." Babette hit him again with the napkin, never looking at him or breaking stride in her conversation with Brigitte.

He and I both had to laugh at her action. It really did seem that these two girls might as well have been American, the way they were acting. It also was pretty apparent that the girls were close, and they were enjoying themselves.

"Hey," Elvis leaned over even further, lowering his voice even more. "As we were walking over to the restaurant, Babette told me Brigitte was really excited. She thinks you're cute...plus you're a doctor!"

That embarrassed me a little. After all, why weren't they squealing, jumping up and down because they were with Elvis Presley? It was flattering that Brigitte had noticed me at all. I told him, "She's pretty, and you've done me a big favor but...I think they both would be gaga over you.... after all, you're Elvis."

He kind of sneered his lip playfully. "Not now I'm not.... I'm just an impressionist trying to make an honest living." He took a big sip of water and looked at me as he swallowed it.

For a second...just a fleeting moment, I think I saw a touch of sadness, maybe a touch of regret. It lasted only momentarily, and I wasn't sure that was what I had seen at all, but for an instant I thought he missed his former life as he was talking of his new life. Maybe he would eventually open up to me and tell me everything. Maybe.

"Here we are...shrimp," the waitress said in a heavy French accent placing a large plate in front of me.

"Merci beaucoup," I gave my French thank you my best shot.

"Very good!" Babette and Brigitte chimed in and applauded my effort to speak French.

Elvis Is Alive

Everyone "oohed" and "aaahed" over their meals and immediately began to dig in. I had to tease Brigitte. Her squid didn't look appetizing at all! She forked up a big helping and pushed it in front of my face.

"*Mangez-vous*. Eat." she said.

I had to be impolite. I turned up my nose and refused. She laughed and shrugged her shoulders as she took a big bite.

I had to admit my stomach turned just a second. I thought her meal looked terrible, but she seemed to relish it!

"How's your shrimp?" Elvis asked.

"Great!" I said, and I wasn't kidding. I had come to appreciate the French way of spicing their food. Even though this was Monaco, the French influence was obvious and I loved it.

"*Mon ami*, Elvis!" A loud, heavily Italian-accented voice rang out across the room.

Elvis looked up from his meal. He immediately broke out in a big smile, jumped up from the table and strode to meet a short, balding man with a big handshake.

"Alfonso Bugatti, how good to see you again!"

The two men slapped each other on the back heartily and hugged each other. Obviously, this was the heir to the Bugatti automobile fortune. He was the owner of *The Wandering Lady*, the magnificent yacht where we were going to party later that night. He and Elvis appeared to be great friends.

Alfonso was accompanied by one of the tallest blondes I had ever seen. She was dressed in a skin-tone Spandex body suit. She wore beautiful jewelry and would obviously be the center of attention wherever she went.

Alfonso and Elvis were having a great time. They were speaking in English, although Elvis had to talk very slowly, loudly, and deliberately for his Italian friend to understand.

I took my eyes away from the statuesque blonde and returned my attention to our table. Babette and Brigitte were looking at Alfonso's companion with tilted eyebrows. Uh oh.... I knew what that meant.

Elvis eventually brought Alfonso over to the table. The blonde dutifully remained slightly behind her Italian companion.

"Dr. St. John, I want you to meet a good friend of mine, Alfonso Bugatti." Elvis held out his arm. "And this is Angelique."

I got up and shook the Italian millionaire's hand. Angelique wasn't as tall as I had imagined; this guy was just that short. His bald head shone brightly as I shook his small hand.

"Very well to meet you," he stumbled along in thick Italian. His smile was genuine and infectious. The strength of his handshake was honest.

He didn't have much in the way of looks, but he was the type of fellow who made you like him immediately. Angelique was probably with him only for his money and because of his last name, Bugatti. But I didn't feel bad for him, nor did I begrudge his wealth. He was that nice!

"Nice to meet you, Mr. Bugatti." I didn't know what else to say.

"Puhlease," he answered. His accent made his English very difficult to understand.

"Call me, Alfonso!" he continued. He was so enthusiastic in his introduction that I didn't want to attempt to correct his convoluted English. Since I knew no Italian, it was obvious that we would have to communicate in the best way we could.

"I want all of you to come to my yacht tonight. We will have a big party," he exclaimed.

I looked at the group. The girls seemed to understand the invitation but were reluctant to accept it.

Elvis was very excited about the invitation. He had been on the boat before and knew how nice it was.

"I'd love to come," I said. "I mean, if everyone else does."

Mr. Bugatti picked up a glass on the table and held it up in a seeming salute to everyone.

"Good, very well...good. We will expect you then in a few hours. After you complete your dinner." His accent prevented every word from being understood clearly, but his enthusiasm was obvious.

Elvis patted him on the back. "We'll be there right after we finish our meal."

Brigitte and Babette weren't very enthused. They looked at Angelique and then back to each other.

Alfonso clapped his hands together with pleasure at our accepting his invitation and then grabbed Angelique by the elbow. They turned, this "Mutt and Jeff" couple, and headed out the entrance. Alfonso turned and waved as they slipped out the door.

Elvis turned to the table and sat down.

Babette looked at him. "I like your friend Alfonso," she said, "but I don't know if Brigitte and I like the big tall lady. She wears too much make-up."

Brigitte said, "I agree." Her eyes grew big as she looked at me, expecting me to agree as well.

Elvis looked at me. He hesitated slightly before he said anything, then cleared his throat.

"Robert and I agree with you. Angelique is overdressed. I don't mean to be rude to her behind her back...but she's probably from a very poor family and doesn't have the ability to look as attractive as you two. Do you understand?"

They looked at him curiously, awaiting his further denouncements of the blonde vixen.

"It's just that Alfonso Bugatti is such a nice man. He's a good friend of mine. I don't think we should hold his poor taste in women against him and not go to his party. Not everyone is as lucky as Dr. St. John and I are to have such exquisite taste in women and the good fortune to be seen with such beautiful women as you. Alfonso is very rich, but look at him. He probably has to go out with whoever will have him, even if it is someone who's as disadvantaged as his poor girlfriend."

Both girls stretched their necks and clucked their approval of his assessment of the situation.

I've seen some marvelous politicians in my day, but the speech I had just witnessed was without equal. He had just convinced the two girls that one of the most stunning women I had ever seen was a dog. We all returned to our meals. The girls probably knew what he had said about Angelique wasn't true, but he sure told them what they wanted to hear. Yes, Elvis knew how to handle women.

I watched him closely for a few minutes, attempting to catch his eye. He glanced at me when the girls weren't looking and gave me a big wink.

The girls had nothing to fear from Angelique. They were just as beautiful, but in a less provocative way. Her presence was no reason why we shouldn't be able to go to the largest yacht in Monaco and party with the elite and the beautiful. He had identified the jealousy that was as thick as it could be and defused it. I chuckled to myself. We would have a great time tonight. When I felt it was safe, I slipped him a grateful smile.

Robert Mickey Maughon, M.D.

Chapter Ten

We decided to go back to the hotel to get ready for the party and to wait to go to the casino the following night. By the end of the meal, the girls were excitedly discussing what they would wear. We hurried back to the hotel. Elvis and I decided to wear lightweight suits. Babette and Brigitte huddled in his suite trying on different outfits and changing their hair.

Finally we were dressed and ready to go. The girls looked fresh and glamorous. Elvis and I looked debonair, or at least we thought so. By the time we had gotten dressed and ready, it was about nine p.m.

The lights of Monte Carlo shimmered out on the sea. Alfonso's yacht was brillantly lit up. It was the largest one in the marina and the most impressive. The blaring music could be heard all along the waterfront. The most dressed-up people were passing us apparently heading to the casino. We found ourselves with a younger, "hipper" crowd as we followed the sea to the pier.

A loud, pulsating disco beat emanated from the top deck of the ship. "The Wandering Lady" was one of the premier personal vessels in the Mediterranean. Elvis explained that it was an essential part of Alfonso's image as an European playboy. In Italy, and throughout Europe, the sons of prominent industrial families were expected to uphold certain images: wild parties, beautiful exotic women...let the good times roll. Alfonso Bugatti tried to uphold all of those ideals. He surrounded himself with beautiful people, and he positioned himself in all the right places, Monte Carlo being the ritziest and most exalted. His yacht was the hub of a young group that jetted around Europe in pursuit of fun. Alfonso Bugatti supposedly was the epitome of this privileged class.

We met another "dressed-to-the-nines" couple and walked with them to the boat. Two large uniformed guards inspected us at the entrance of the yacht. We were immediately escorted inside.

I was astonished. This was more than a yacht. It was a mansion afloat: luxurious woods, crystal chandeliers, total elegance. The yacht definitely was going to be the gathering place for the crowd after they left the casino.

Elvis led us upstairs toward the pulsating music. Disco strobe lights blinked and flashed over the top deck. The whole deck had been covered with a cotton linen canopy, which magnified the light and intensified the music. More than a hundred people were dancing. Some wore dresses and evening clothes, and others were in casual designer clothes. They all were moving wildly with the music.

Elvis and I spotted Angelique by the back rail. She had piled her long blonde tresses on top of her head. She towered above everyone else.

"Wherever she is, I'm sure Alfonso is close by," Elvis yelled in my ear, trying to be heard above the music.

We pulled the girls close and began to push our way through the crowd to the back rail. They were packed in so closely that it was difficult to make progress. Their gyrations occasionally sent one of them bumping into us. Eventually, we made it to the back.

Alfonso was talking to a dark Latin type who was dressed in an expensive black silk suit. Angelique was beautiful in a sequined dress. She stood along the railing, looking back over the sea.

"Hey, my American friends." Alfonso seemed happy to see us.

Babette and Brigitte suspiciously eyed Angelique as she swayed to the music.

"This is Antonio." Alfonso introduced Elvis and me to his friend. We shook hands with the stranger. He said something to Elvis, but the music was so loud that I couldn't overhear what was being said.

Alfonso yelled above the loud music. "Let's all go downstairs to the state room. We can have our own private party there."

Elvis and I looked at each other and nodded our heads in agreement. The lights were too bright and the music too loud up on the deck for my blood. The girls were already dancing together. Elvis shouted in their ears and they agreed to follow us.

We made the same arduous journey back through the celebrating throng. Disco had died out in America, but in Europe it was still going strong. The crowd of dancers seemed to be having a blast. A few of the female partiers had even taken off their tops.

We had to push and shove our way to go even a few feet. Eventually we made it back to the stateroom door. I glanced back at the mass of humanity. These people loved to dance and party.

We walked downstairs. Alfonso led us through the foyer to what I assume was the stateroom. Intricately carved mahogany panels lined the walls. A dinner table dominated the center of the room. Small gold porpoises adorned its legs at each corner.

The Mediterranean was picturesque in all of its grandeur through a large state window. We could see the flash of the strobe lights as if flashes of lightning were jumping off the deck above us. Strangely, the noise was muffled here. Considering the quality of the construction, I assumed the walls had been insulated against loud sounds.

Babette and Brigitte took leave of the group and stood at the far corner of the room. They seemed to be enjoying themselves looking out of the window and occasionally dancing to the barely audible music from above.

Angelique swayed to the music slightly. She stood behind the men at the far side of the window. Her tall figure was outlined against the dim light of the night. I looked around. Elvis, Alfonso and Antonio were all staring at her. She was a beautiful sight to see.

I looked back around. Elvis and Alfonso seemed to be in an intense conversation. Antonio was sitting at the table. He extracted a white napkin. He unrolled it and laid its contents on the table: a small straw, a silver thimble spoon and a foil wrap.

I turned to Elvis. His arms were folded across his chest. I looked down the table to Brigitte and Babette. They were busy in conversation as they continued dancing to the music. The lighting in the stateroom was very dim. I doubted they could see what was being spread out on the table in front of us.

My attention returned to Antonio and Alfonso at the table. Angelique dashed from her position at the other end of the room and hovered excitedly above the two men. Antonio slowly unfolded the foil.

Cocaine!

I wrenched around. I wanted to see Elvis' reaction. He had never been rumored to be associated with drugs like cocaine. Elvis still held his position with his arms crossed over his chest. It was apparent that he was not very happy with the scene unfolding in front of him.

We were in the domicile of Alfonso. I agreed with Elvis' posture. I wasn't too pleased either. We could leave if we didn't like it. But it wasn't our place to tell a man what he could or couldn't do in the privacy of his own property, especially since we were in Europe. We were a very long way from the good old U.S. of A.

Elvis' defensive posture in regard to the drug spoke volumes, and his actions now spoke louder than words.

Angelique picked up the small spoon and took a scoop of the powder. She held one nostril closed and 'snorted' with the other. She closed her eyes and shivered. Afterward, with closed eyes, she wiped the remnants of the white substance from her nostrils.

Antonio and Alfonso turned to me, offering the next 'hit' if I wanted it. I held up my hand in protest and smiled, politely declining. They then turned to Elvis. He also smiled slightly, shaking his head and holding up his hand to decline.

Antonio and Alfonso looked at each other and shrugged in a "who cares" gesture.

Angelique had moved back to her place at the end of the room. She resumed her rhythmic movement to the dampened music. Her tall, lithe figure danced its own dance. She seemed oblivious to anyone or anything.

Antonio reached for the small straw. He raked out a small portion of the cocaine and smoothed a line on the table. He poised the straw against his right nostril, squeezed the other off and inhaled deeply. His eyes rolled back in his head, as he leaned the entire weight of his body against the back of the chair. A slow smile spread across his face. He looked at me and opened his eyes, then handed the straw to me. I took it and placed it back down on the table.

Alfonso came from behind him and picked up the straw. He followed the same ritual. He scraped a small portion of the whiteness on the shiny table top. He spread a neat, thin line. Alfonso bent over and snorted. His face blanched as he straightened up. With his eyes glazed over, he turned to Elvis and extended the small straw to him. Elvis again politely declined. He smiled at Alfonso, but it was obvious that he did not agree with his friend's actions and was not going to participate in taking the drug.

Alfonso put his hand on Elvis' shoulder and patted it reassuringly. He said something in his thick Italian accent. His small bald head was extremely shiny in the dim light. Alfonso leaned over as if to whisper something to Elvis, and then collapsed.

Alfonso lay sprawled before our feet. It seemed like an eternity before I realized that the man wasn't pulling some kind of practical joke.

I looked up at Elvis. He looked at me. We were both wide-eyed.

"Alfonso. Alfonso!" I yelled.

I jumped up and hovered over him. Instinctively I reached for his carotid artery. There was no pulse in his neck.

"He's had an M.I. He's had a heart attack!" I shouted.

Antonio jumped from his chair and ran toward the door. What a friend, I thought.

The pusher fled from the room in this time of emergency. I pulled Alfonso's lifeless body on to his back and immediately began CPR. He had already begun to turn cyanotic. I motioned for Elvis to help me. I glimpsed Angelique swaying to the vibrations of the music from above. She was oblivious to the danger her boyfriend was in.

"What should I do?" Elvis quizzed as he bent over his friend's body.

I continued to pump Alfonso's chest. After every fourth beat, I opened his mouth and breathed in.

"Here." I placed Elvis' hands over Alfonso's chest and instructed him to rhythmically press down, replacing the vital function of his heart.

Babette and Brigitte now joined us. Elvis yelled at them to get help, and they ran helter skelter out of the room.

In America we are blessed with a marvelously effective system for dealing with emergencies such as this. We call 911 and are instantly connected with an emergency response team. I was not sure how this worked in Europe but hoped the girls would know how to contact a similar service.

I continued my CPR efforts. I wished we had a cardiac monitor with a defibrillation unit. The way Alfonso looked, I didn't feel good about his chances. I couldn't get a pulse from him and he wasn't breathing on his own.

Angelique finally noticed the commotion. She walked across the room, hovering above us. She held her hands across her mouth in utter shock and appeared to tremble.

Finally the doors burst open to the room. Several white-uniformed men brought in a stretcher. They didn't have a cardiac monitor.

"Let's get him on the gurney," I ordered. We shoved and pulled Alfonso's body onto the collapsible stretcher. I continued my resuscitative efforts as we wheeled him off the boat. I could hear gasps and muffled words from the crowd as we left the yacht.

The ambulance was located at the end of the pier. It did not take long for us to reach it after the paramedics arrived. The interval of time from when Alfonso had been stricken to their arrival was critical. We hooked him up to the monitor in the ambulance.

"Nothing...flat line." I grabbed the paddles of the defibrillating unit.

"Clear!" I screamed. I guess the urgency in my voice was understood by everyone. All of the personnel instantly backed off.

Thwumph. One-hundred-fifty joules of electrical current surged through his body.

"Nothing," I declared, as I still could not find a pulse. A paramedic was trying to start an IV. Out of the corner of my eye, I could see the tall figure of Angelique being supported by Babette and Brigitte.

"Clear!" I yelled again.

Thwumph. This time two-hunded joules of electricity surged through his body. Still no pulse.

"Let's go!" I motioned at the ambulance driver to get to the hospital. The ER there would be better equipped to handle this emergency than we were. The paramedic who was trying to intubate Alfonso had been unsuccessful. As the ambulance driver prepared to leave for the hospital, Angelique, Babette and Brigitte jumped into the back of the ambulance.

Angelique was crying hysterically. Her tall frame trembled. Babette and Brigitte held her closely and did their best to reassure her.

We did our best to try to save Alfonso. I eventually had to intubate him myself. Although I was now a pathologist, I had been an ER doc for so long that I felt I could intubate anyone. However, his short stature made it difficult to get the tube into his trachea.

We sped to the hospital, which was not far from the casino. Like many European cities, the hospital is located downtown. We frantically continued our resuscitation efforts as the siren blared loudly. I was finally able to give Alfonso a large bolus of epinephrine. His heart would not respond.

When we reached the hospital, a large contingent of emergency room personnel swarmed the ambulance. They essentially took over the resuscitative effort. Evidently the word had reached them that this was Alfonso Bugatti. I was exhausted and was glad to allow the ER doctors to take over.

Elvis Is Alive

Elvis was sweating like crazy. He was obviously exhausted, as was I. That didn't prevent him from taking the time to thank the emergency personnel for their help in trying to save his friend. The girls took Angelique aside and continued to try to comfort her.

I had not run a cardiac code in many years. I felt sure it would take a miracle to save Alfonso's life. His heart had shown no signs of life despite all our efforts. If the Monte Carlo Emergency Room personnel could save him, my hat would be off to their heroic effort.

"How does it look?" Elvis walked over to me, a look of fatigue and worry etched all over his face.

"I doubt he'll make it, it doesn't look good." I whispered in his ear as the three girls were in range of my voice.

He shook his head glumly in acknowledgment. We both glanced over at the distraught Angelique. Her beauty was only accentuated by her grief. She was sincerely upset by this horrible turn of events.

Babette and Brigitte's concern for her made me want to hug both of them in appreciation.

"Monsieur, monsieur." A young man, I assumed to be a doctor, came directly to Elvis and me. He whispered something in Elvis' ear.

"He's gone." Elvis turned to me, his voice racked with emotion.

"Damn cocaine!" he mumbled.

He reluctantly strode over to Angelique, bent over and whispered the bad news to her. She immediately covered her face with her hands and began to weep bitterly. Babette and Brigitte began to cry and hugged her.

The mascara began to run down all of their faces.

Elvis walked back to me and stood silently. His jaw set firmly. "When I see that Antonio guy," he seethed.

"Elvis, that won't help anything." I put my hand on my friend's shoulder. We both stood there in silence. What had started out as a wonderfully exciting evening had ended in tragedy.

It was a somber group that headed back to our hotel. The walk was gloomy and dreadful. Oh, how only a few hours can change things.

Angelique declined our invitation to join us back at the hotel.

The girls were sincerely concerned about her. They hugged Angelique and asked her what they could do. She apparently did not want to leave the body. Babette said later that Angelique would go with the Bugatti entourage back to Italy. It turned out that Angelique was Alfonso's sister.

Elvis felt especially bad. He felt he should have protested to the cocaine use. He didn't know that drugs would be brought out when they went downstairs to the stateroom. He had thought they were simply going down to visit in a quieter setting.

"Yeah, and wasn't that Antonio a snake!" I exclaimed.

"Provided bad cocaine and ran out when his friend died." Elvis shook his head.

"Should we go to the police?" I asked.

Elvis shook his head in bewilderment. For the first time since I had known him, he seemed at a loss.

"I don't know what to do. I don't want Angelique to get into trouble, but someone needs to stop that guy! I say we have one of the girls call the police. She won't be looked at as a foreigner. She could describe him and maybe he'll get caught."

I nodded in agreement. "Yeah, I think that's what we need to do. It makes sense."

"When we get to the room, I'll have Babette call," Elvis said.

We continued a slow walk back to the hotel. When we got there, the first thing Elvis did was explain to Babette that he wanted her to make an anonymous call to the police. She wholeheartedly agreed. We all congregated in the master suite.

Babette did a good job of explaining what happened and describing Antonio. She politely refused the police request to come in and make a statement. Babette explained when she was off the phone that the police knew who Antonio was. Evidently he was notorious in this part of the world. They also seemed none too surprised that Alfonso was caught up in something like this. Cocaine was a part of the scene in Europe, especially at these parties.

Babette told the police we would keep up with the case through the newspapers. If Antonio was not prosecuted, we would come forward to testify. The police weren't satisfied with that, but we had done our duty, sort of. Although we all felt better after calling the police, it was a sad group that readied for bed.

"Do you think we're doing the right thing?" I asked.

"I know how difficult the police here can be," Elvis said. "The girls didn't even know that cocaine was at the party. They were talking in the corner of the room, remember? I don't think it would be fair to involve them in this, do you?"

"No, I honestly don't."

"Let's see how things go. We can follow this in the papers. From what the police told Babette, they'll get Antonio."

The girls had gone into the other rooms. Elvis and I sat silently by a table near the window. *The Wandering Lady* was eerily quiet. The tragedy had stopped the party. Without the lights and the music from the yacht, Monte Carlo seemed hauntingly still.

We sat there, not uttering a word. The night breeze ruffled our hair and filled our nostrils with the smell of salt air.

"Let's go on a trip tomorrow," Elvis finally remarked, after about ten minutes of strained silence. "Monte Carlo won't be any fun after tonight." He looked at me with saddened eyes.

"Okay. I'm here at your invitation. Whatever you say."

I was about to speak again when he interrupted.

"You know why you came to see me, Dr. St John?"

"Yes..." I responded hesitatingly.

"I want to tell you the whole story...my whole story."

There was a continued sadness to his eyes and voice.

I had made up my mind not to push it, and I began to explain that. "Elvis, I've decided not to ask you all of that stuff. I've grown to cherish your friendship. Whatever your reasons, they're none of my business!"

He smiled that smile with just a hint of upturned lip.

"Tonight has changed my mind. After you told me some of the things that had happened back home, I made up my mind last week not to tell you anything further. But now..." he hesitated. The smile slipped from his face.

"After seeing what happened to Alfonso..." His smile now turned to a frown. He held up his right hand and snapped his fingers.

"Life can be taken from someone so quickly. I think I want my story to be told. I know I want someone to write down what happened and what made me do what I did."

I sat there silently. I had found Elvis Presley, and he was going to spill his guts to me.

"Of course, you have to keep you're part of the bargain." His face lit up and his smile returned.

"What do you mean?"

"You know our agreement: you tell me how you came to find me, and I'll fill you in on my..." he hesitated and groped for the right words, "my journey," he concluded.

We smiled at each other. I reached out and shook his hand.

"All right," I agreed.

"Let's get a good night's sleep, and we'll take off tomorrow for Paris." He smiled. It was the first real smile I had seen since the tragedy earlier in the evening.

"What's so funny?" I blurted out, as his smile had become a broad grin.

"I'm going to take you on a trip to Paris. It will be fun, a long roundabout trip. We have to leave this tragedy behind us. We'll take the girls with us and have a good time."

"Okay," I responded. "Sounds good to me."

Elvis jumped up from where we were sitting and said he was going to tell Babette and Brigitte to get ready. A moment later I heard voices from the next room.

I felt excited too. Poor Alfonso and Angelique Bugatti. From their family tragedy, a wish of mine would come true. I looked forward to the next day with great anticipation and excitement.

Chapter Eleven

The night passed quickly for me as the events of the evening had exhausted me. I was awakened by the warm body of Brigitte snuggling into bed next to me. I think she had slept in the adjacent room. I'm not sure where she came from.

We didn't make love, but her kisses were so passionate that I knew sometime in the near future we would become lovers.

"I feel like such a lucky guy," I told her.

"You should," she responded smugly as she kissed me again.

"Hey, what are you guys up to?" The laughing voice of Elvis came from the door. Brigitte jumped up like a shot out of a gun.

"Mon Dieu!" she exclaimed and ran out of the room.

Elvis and I laughed loudly as she headed out the door.

"Are you ready to go?" he asked.

"Sure," I said. I got out of bed.

"We're going to take the Orient Express."

"Hey, that's something I've always wanted to do!"

He and I shared more small talk and made plans

about the trip. We would load the Peugeot and head north where we would then meet a connecting train in Venice, Italy.

The road to Venice was narrow and winding with spectacular mountainous terrain at several places. Under the circumstances, it was good that we had left town. Elvis was obviously upset by the death of Alfonso. I guess he had seen enough tragedy in his life. For that matter, so had I.

When we started out, Elvis drove and I sat in front with him, while the girls chatted in the back. The trip wasn't as tedious as I had thought it would be. The little car trudged over the blacktop, making its way for the train that would lead us to the past. I looked forward to the passage on this train, as I felt sure that was where Elvis would tell me his story. There's something about the constant clanking of the train against the track that settles one's nerves. The swaying of the train and the noise usually is a conducement to open up and talk about things that might otherwise stay hidden in the past.

Elvis and I took turns driving. We stopped at little roadside stands and ate hearty pasta and sausage.

When I drove, Elvis and Babette would sit in the back. When he drove, Brigitte and I would. Brigitte and I kissed a lot and tried to get to know each other better. The cramped Peugeot wasn't the best place for two people to get to know each other, but we tried anyway. Meanwhile, Babette and Elvis acted like an old married couple.

We took the road to Verona and stayed overnight. The old hotel where we stayed was clean and comfortable. Brigitte and Babette stayed in one room, Elvis and I in another. Brigitte and I were not ready to be intimate.

We left Verona and headed for our goal: Hotel Cipriani, in Venice. We were going to spend a few days at this old Venetian symbol before taking the Orient Express across Austria, Switzerland and France and ultimately returning to Paris.

We pulled into the parking lot at the Cipriani. The bellman took our bags and the valet parked our car. This hotel was one of the old classics. We again were greeted by the concierge. Elvis seemed to know everybody.

Finally, Brigitte and I decided to take a room together. It wasn't a conscious decision; it just happened. Elvis and Babette's luggage was taken to one room, and ours was taken to the room next door.

We decided to take in the sights of the canals on a gondola. It was quite romantic, two couples cruising the waterways of this water-bound city in separate boats. We even had the drivers race each other in the crowded grand canal.

I recommend that any person who goes to Venice take the gondola at sundown and extend the ride into nighttime. There's no better way to get close to someone than to be snuggled up close as you glide through Venice on these special boats. I could feel Brigitte's desire emanate from her as we circumnavigated the city over its historic waterways.

We had a remarkable meal right in the gondola that night. We glided up to a small Venetian restaurant, ordered cheese, wine, and fresh loaves of hot bread. It was as if we were at a McDonald's on the water. Afterward, we just floated away.

When we returned to Hotel Cipriano that evening, Elvis and Babette disappeared into their room. They said good-night courteously enough, but it was apparent they had had enough of our company. They wanted to be alone.

Brigitte and I walked around to the large hotel pool. We were the only people there. The Italian moonlight reflected furiously off the crystal clear water. I looked into Brigitte's eyes. We kissed long and hard. Before I knew it we slipped into the pool naked. This might seem inappropriate in the U.S., but in *l'Europa, c'est la vie.*

We made love in the silvery, watery bed. I feared that someone would walk up and see us, but no one did. Afterward, we ran laughing to our room. We had not brought towels and water dripped from us as if it had been raining.

We sneaked by Elvis and Babette's room. The lights were off and I had not heard anything. We stepped as silently as we could into our room. We made love again in the soft feather bed. Exhausted, we fell asleep in each other's arms.

I awoke with a start after a horrible dream. A sense of dread came over me. I reached over to make sure Brigitte was okay. Perspiring, I realized where I was, got up and showered. I slowly washed the sense of forboding away, watching it swirl down the drain. I thought momentarily about Marcia, but her memory faded too. I returned to bed and snuggled close to Brigitte.

It was mid-morning when I awoke. Brigitte was still curled up in bed, sleeping with a smile etched on her small face. I looked out our window and marveled at how this city functioned with its watery byways.

Elvis Is Alive

No city in North America has roadways any more congested than the traffic lanes of Venice. It's just most places in the world use automobiles, whereas the Venetians use floating vessels.

Knock! Knock! Knock! A pounding came at the door. I looked at Brigitte. She stirred slightly but did not awaken at the initial noise. Then the knocking became a desperate, constant battering sound. By the time I had answered, Brigitte was awake.

"All right, all right, hold your horses," I yelled as I ran to the door and opened it.

The hysterical form of Babette pushed past me and collapsed on the bed with Brigitte. Tears ran down her face and she trembled. Both girls were speaking as quickly as they could in French, with an occasional English word.

I tried to understand the words they were saying.

"He doesn't love me, Brigitte." Babette said boldly.

"Non, non, Babette, Elvis loves you." Brigitte tried to reassure her cousin.

Before I knew it, Brigitte was packing her bags.

"What is wrong?" I pulled Brigitte over to me. She pulled away in a manner that hurt my feelings. I had done nothing wrong.

The next thing I knew the two of them had their bags together. Brigitte came up and kissed me on the cheek.

"What in the world is wrong?" I was flabbergasted.

"Oh Robert, Elvis has treated Babette badly." Brigitte began crying also.

"We are taking the car and going to see Pierre at the beach house. I'm sorry, but I'm going with her. Please don't be angry with me."

"I don't understand," I sputtered. I tried to grab Brigitte and hold her. She pulled away from me.

"Elvis refuses to marry my beautiful cousin. We are leaving!" With that the two girls scurried out of the room and ran down the hall. A bellman met them at the elevator and helped them carry their luggage downstairs.

I stood with my mouth open at this sudden turn of events. "Women!" I spoke out loud. I finally walked over to Elvis' room across the hall.

I knocked. No response. I knocked again.

"Who is it?" The unmistakable voice of Elvis passed through the door.

"Elvis, it's me, Dr. St. John! May I come in?"

The lock clicked and he opened the door.

"What happened?" I asked.

"She didn't like something I said," he answered as he welcomed me into the room. He didn't appear upset, but simply walked back over to the bed and sat down. The TV was on some kind of Italian soap opera. He sat on the bed and stared blankly at the set. Images of men and women in love paraded across the screen. It strangely reminded me of the situation I had just been through.

"She wanted me to marry her," he continued, not looking up from the TV.

"What did you say to upset her that much?"

"I told her that there was someone in my past who could never be replaced. She doesn't know who Priscilla is, of course. Hell, she doesn't even know who I really AM!"

I sat there not knowing what to say or do. He finally looked up from the TV again. A large tear formed in his right eye and rolled down his cheek.

"Will you still take the Orient Express back to Paris with me?"

"Of course I will," I answered.

"Good." He wiped the tear from his face.

"After all," I continued, "what are friends for?"

"Good, Doc. We'll go tomorrow as we had planned."

Elvis didn't say much the rest of the day. It was pleasant sitting out by the pool, but I missed the girls' company. Of course I didn't tell Elvis this. We swam and passed the time. The Italian sun felt different than any I had felt anywhere before. It was bright but didn't burn. If we had been at a higher altitude I could have explained it, but Venice is as close to sea level as you can get.

Elvis needed Babette, but he obviously wasn't over Priscilla. How strange it all seemed. Why did he stay away from the U.S. if he still loved his wife? I had a thousand and one questions to ask him.

From what I could see, Elvis had a million reasons to return to his former life. He seemingly had very little reason to stay here.

The sun burned itself into my soul as I wrestled with all these questions. Fair was fair, though. He had said he would explain things to me, and I believed he would. But, as all good friends know, it's best not to pry. It's better to be polite.

Elvis didn't seem as upset about Babette leaving as I did about losing Brigitte. I felt that the situation was probably only temporary, but who knew? What if Babette had left him for good? What if her leaving had made him change his mind about telling me everything? He was known for being moody.

Early in the afternoon, I cleared my throat to pick up where I had left off in my story. I hesitated.

Something told me that I should bide my time, that the Orient Express was my best bet. I had a gut feeling that the mesmerizing action of the train would make anyone open up, especially if that person had the story of Elvis Aron Presley to tell.

I decided that if he didn't tell me everything by the time we returned to Paris, I would return home and let the story stay forever with him.

It was time for Dr. Robert St. John to find out the truth or go home. I wasn't going to twist his arm to make him tell me. Elvis Presley was his own man. If he wanted to tell me his story, he would tell me of his own volition.

As the saying goes in Venice, things happen for circumstances, accident, or incident.

Chapter Twelve

"I miss the girls!" I exclaimed as we boarded the beautifully decorated Pullman car that would house us on the trip to Paris.

He looked at me with sad eyes, and I instantly regretted opening my mouth as we boarded the train.

"Sorry," he began to explain. "They'll be with us again. I just can't promise Babette I'll marry her while I still feel the way I do about Priscilla." He sighed deeply as he tossed the last of his bags onto the storage rack.

"I didn't mean to say that," I muttered. I turned a reddish shade as embarrassment crept up into my face. "I didn't mean to get so personal," I continued in such a hushed voice that I wasn't sure he could even hear me.

We settled in. The conductor came around and prepared us to leave, just as in the Agatha Christie novel.

The air was strained between Elvis and me. I'm sure he felt that I was waiting only for him to tell me his story. I *was* curious, but I was much more interested now in being a good, supportive friend to him, the kind he had needed back home in his former life: the kind of friend who might have prevented his drug addiction and also helped with some of the horrible loneliness he must have felt.

The tension was so thick that I finally blurted out, "Elvis, you don't have to tell me your life's story. I just want to be your friend."

He looked at me with a confused expression. "What?"

"I want to be your friend first. Sure, I'd like to know your story, but only if you want to tell me. There, I said it!" I felt a huge burden lift from my shoulders.

He laughed that laugh that I had heard a hundred times over the past week or so. "Dr. St. John, I've just been sitting here worrying about Babette and thinking about Priscilla and Lisa Marie. I'm going to tell you my story. I told you I would." He smiled at me.

"I'm even going to ask your advice about Babette." He laughed again.

I smiled back at him and looked outside our car at the people milling around the Venice depot. Slowly we pulled out of the station. The train gradually but methodically increased its speed as we eased into the lovely Italian countryside. We would backtrack to Verona, the city we had driven through, and then head north to Vienna and Switzerland.

I held my breath. He was finally going to explain everything. I couldn't believe it. I hesitated looking at him for fear that I would break the mood he was in.

I guess famous people don't realize how we mere mortals are sometimes star-struck in their presence. Elvis seemingly still didn't understand this.

Elvis Is Alive

I imagined I would have to resume my story where I had left off in Memphis. I stared out the window and started trying to remember all the facts. I just wished Brigitte and Babette were here. Women always seem to make everything okay. Don't ask me why. For some reason, I felt they would make our trip and conversation perfect.

The conductor checked with us several times. We could eat in the dining car or we could have room service.

"How about some coffee?" Elvis asked.

"Sounds good to me."

He pulled on the cord in the sitting area of our sleeper. Almost immediately a waiter appeared.

"What would you like?" Elvis asked.

"I don't know. What kind are you getting?"

"Let's get the African blend we drank in the little restaurant in Paris when we first met."

Elvis said something quickly in French to the dark-skinned waiter, who nodded enthusiastically and headed off, evidently in search of our coffee.

"You know what, Doc?"

"What?" I asked.

"I miss the girls, but we'll have a lot more time to talk this way." He waved his hand over the empty car. "I might be reluctant to talk in front of Babette. Actually, I think she understands English perfectly, no matter what she says."

"I thought so." I said, and nodded in acknowledgment. We sat in silence as we awaited our coffee.

The Italian landscape whizzed by. The coastal terrain of Vienna slowly gave way to a hilly landscape as we headed west to Verona. I continued to sort my thoughts. The last conversation we had

had concerning my journey to find him had precipitated the move to the beach house. I had left off when Dr. Regent and the governor were approaching me about the dilemma concerning the Presley estate.

I wasn't sure what part of the conversation had bothered him the most: the part about the royalty controversy or my bringing up Priscilla. Since then I had discovered he still had very strong feelings for her.

We had a lot of ground to cover. How would he react to all of the references to his family I would be making? I now saw the benefit of not having the girls around for this. In reality they would be a distraction. We would make much more progress being alone on the train together.

I allowed myself to think back over the last year in detail. Perhaps I should take notes and make an outline? No, I would just do the best I could and see where it led me.

I felt my heart begin to beat a little faster. Why was I nervous? I looked over at Elvis. He was sitting and looking out the window at the Italian landscape. What thoughts were going through his mind? I had no idea. How well did I really know him anyway?

I felt my palms getting sweaty. I had to be realistic. If he didn't tell me everything in the next few days, I would have to go home empty-handed. I wasn't wealthy. My money was almost gone.

Sure, Elvis had been very generous on this excursion across Europe, but afterward, I would have to go home and work. If I didn't get his story now, my journey was over. Even if my mission was a failure, I wouldn't have missed this adventure for anything in the world.

Elvis Is Alive

I again resolved that he was going to have to tell me his story without my asking him. That decision made me anxious. What if I had given up a year of my life to follow him, gotten so close, and still did not get the story?

Thankfully the waiter returned with our coffee. He brought it to us on an ornate silver service that appeared to be a Moorish antique. This is what I adored about the Orient Express, its total class and elegance.

"Where should we start?" Elvis asked as he poured some coffee.

I reached over and took a cup. My hand shook slightly.

Suddenly, the train swayed to left as we rounded a curve,

"Why don't we start where we left off?" I offered, as we both took a sip of the dark rich liquid.

I thought back to the day when Governor Rex Chambers told me the incredible story of Winston Doyle and his plan to exhume Elvis Presley's grave to see if the body was there.

The story I was to tell demonstrated how low people would stoop to get money. They would grovel, and I mean *grovel* to get it. But I guess Elvis knew that. He probably knew more about crooked agents and cheating highrollers than I ever would.

The clattering train brought me back to the present. I looked over at Elvis. His jet black hair was framed against the gold tapestry that covered the Pullman's walls. Here I was alone with "the King." I would attempt to tell my story again.

As the countryside slid by, I gritted my teeth, girded my self-confidence and once again began to recount my story of following him.

* * * * *

"This isn't happening, Dr. Regent. I became a coroner to be a helpful force in society...not to go digging up celebrities and being on TV," I protested.

Governor Chambers laughed at my protestations. His silvery white hair bounced as he laughed. Not a single strand fell out of place. I didn't know if it was hair spray that kept it in place or years of constant grooming and combing.

My face was contorted with concern.

The governor turned to me.

"Dr. St. John, I'm not saying this is going to happen. I'm just a firm believer in covering all the bases. I want to be prepared for all eventualities. I wanted to come and see who you were, what type person you are, that sort of thing. When a lady as beautiful and as popular as Priscilla Presley approaches you for help, well...I don't know many men who wouldn't do everything in their power to try and help."

"Especially in an election year," I muttered under my breath.

"What? Watch your mouth, Doctor," Dr. Regent whispered as he rolled his eyes at me in disapproval. The governor had been too busy looking at himself in the mirror adjusting his hair and discussing the political ramifications of this situation to pay any attention to what I had to say.

Dr. Regent had to play the political card, since the funding for his medical school came from the state house in Nashville. I had been at my job for only a short period of time and didn't have to worry about funding problems, as my department was a joint venture between the city and state. I guess I should have been more understanding of Dr. Regent's position. If I had been in his place, I would have been following the governor's concerns with the same rapt attention that he was.

I tried to be more understanding of my boss, but to dig up the grave of Elvis Aron Presley was unthinkable! I didn't care how much money was involved. Hell, there would be a riot. His fans wouldn't allow it.

The governor droned on about the issue involved, something about a law dating back to President Andrew Jackson's time and the indigenous Cherokee people. It seems that a law was passed during that period that allowed the white man to exhume and confiscate the holy burial sites of the Cherokees. That was the law about which the governor was talking. Evidently the law firm representing DELTA Records was exploiting this antiquated law, which was still on the books. Since a law is the law, this was creating a major problem for the state in general and the governor in particular.

I looked back at Dr. Regent, pointed to my watch and mouthed, "I have an autopsy to perform."

"Wait, Dr. St. John. Hold on. The governor is not through with his explanation of what is happening," Dr. Regent said, trying to be as diplomatic as possible.

The white-haired politician was barely slowing down his staccato speech. He was on a roll, ranting about the problems he faced as governor of Tennessee. He also let it be known that he knew everyone was depending on him.

When it became apparent to the politician that I was not going to be in his audience any longer, he walked over and pumped my hand enthusiastically.

"Thanks for your support, my boy." He shook my hand so hard, it hurt. "Now let me warn you!" He bellowed. "Everything I've told you today is to stay here. This is all conjecture at this point. Surely we can stop of all this nonsense before the first shovel of dirt is turned! We can win this argument if we stick together!"

His animation reminded me of an old Southern preacher at a tent revival. He was very exuberant in his sermon, but he was confusing me. I didn't know what he was talking about. Besides, I was sure that none of this nonsense would come to pass anyway.

Elvis Presley's family deserved every bit of the royalties that were being paid to them. Some idiot wasn't going to be given the okay to do this, or at least that's what common sense seemed to scream from the back of my head.

The governor's hair glistened in front of my face. He was exhausted at the end of his exhortations. Sweat also glistened on his brow. Obviously, he was taking this very seriously. Maybe that's the price one pays for being a politician. It's that one crackpot that you better watch out for.

I still didn't understand exactly what role I was supposed to play if it did come to pass. After all, I would just be a cog in the wheel of justice. There wouldn't be a whole lot I could do about the situation if the court ordered it done. Maybe he wanted me to put as positive of a spin on the situation as I could. I don't know. As I said, the whole thing was confusing, and I had been hit with this out of the blue.

My immediate goal was to get my hand freed from the governor's and get the heck out of Dr. Regents office.

"I'll be in touch my boy!" was the way Rex Chambers let me out of his firm handshake.

"Good meeting you, Governor," was all I could muster as I backed out of Dr. Regent's office.

I waved meekly at Dr. Regent as I spun out into Mrs. Mason's office. I looked at her and made a mock gesture of wiping sweat from my brow as soon as the door was safely closed behind me.

"I know, I know, Dr. St. John," she whispered to me as I was leaving. "Dr. Regent has not known what to do. He has been just as exasperated as you with the whole situation. It's sooo…incredible." She rolled her eyes in exaggerated disbelief.

* * * * *

"Do you want some more coffee?" Elvis interrupted my recitation.

I was so interested in telling the story as accurately as I could that I always got immersed in the monologue I was delivering.

"What happened to the little girl you told me about when we first met in Paris?" he asked.

"That was the autopsy I was performing that day. It was a gruesome case and I hated it. It turned out to be a child abuse case. The stepfather was involved and there had been some mutilation. That's where I went after I left Dr. Regent's office that day. Dr. Cross helped me get through that situation and so did Marcia."

Elvis poured us some more coffee. That wasn't

always easy when the train headed around a curve. It took steady hands, which he had.

"I sometimes wonder why I got into pathology and being a coroner in the first place. I had left emergency medicine. One would think that was hard enough, but I loved solving mysteries, and the knowledge that can be obtained through the autopsy process is impressive; but I think you do pay a price after doing such grueling work for a while. It takes its toll."

Elvis looked at me and nodded in understanding. An eternity seemed to elapse. The train's whistle bellowed overhead. The Orient Express began its lazy meandering that would take us through several countries before reaching Paris. I hoped that Babette and Brigitte would be waiting for us there. For now, Elvis and I had plenty of conversation to occupy our time. After all, when we got to his story, we would be covering his life from 1977 on. A panic crept over me. What if we couldn't cover everything in the little time we had together? Would he give me another opportunity in Paris?

I decided to pick up the tempo and be more aggressive. I took a big gulp of the strong coffee and looked over at him. He was looking out the window at the passing scenery. I took a deep breath and began again.

"Elvis, some of what I'm going to tell you now is from second-hand gossip. I wasn't at the meeting that I'm going to tell you about. I found out about it later."

"So you can't verify everything, right? I guess you basically want me to take this with a grain of salt."

Elvis Is Alive

"That's right. This part of the story was told me by a person who told me on one condition—that I never mention his or her name in connection with this part of the story."

"I see, Dr. St. John. I understand. I won't pry, but I'm curious. Why don't you go ahead now? I'll sit back and continue to enjoy the view and listen to your story."

I started my story again as Elvis put his feet up on the soft leather couch and gazed wistfully out the window.

"Winston Doyle and Governor Chambers met with Giorgio Enricci in Las Vegas the week after I met the governor in Dr. Regent's office. The person who shall remain anonymous was present at this meeting." I looked over at Elvis. His eyes were squeezed closed.

"Go ahead, Dr. St. John, I'm listening." He opened his eyes and looked at me. The manner in which he stared at me gave me a shiver. I can still feel it to this day. He apparently knew what I was about to tell him would hurt, but again, he was determined to hear it anyway.

I began to relay the story of how the Mafia kingpin, Giorgio Enricci, ordered the governor and Winston Doyle to the Mirage in Las Vegas. When they gathered, he demanded that he be repaid every penny that was owed him.

Chapter Thirteen

"Chambers, do you know how much money you owe my family? *Twenty-five million dollars!*" the Sicilian Mafia kingpin bellowed. "You've been elected governor of Tennessee on my family's money!"

The silver-haired politician, never at a loss for words, was now speechless.

Giorgio Enricci shook his fat spaghetti-covered finger at him. "And I want it all back! I don't give a damn how you get it, I want it back. If you can think up a better way other than the one our family lawyers have come up with, then so be it. But we will get our money, every last lira."

"And you!" he screamed at Winston Doyle. "What this crooked politician owes me is nothing, absolutely nothing compared with what you owe me!" The crime boss's face had gone from a ruddy dark tan to a dull crimson. "To the last dime, you will pay me the almost one hundred million dollars that you owe me!"

"My lawyers have told you how to get the Elvis Presley estate to pay you the many, many millions that you owe the Enricci family. Hell, I alone will own the whole Presley estate. I'll own everything that singer had. To get it, all you have to do is dig

Elvis Is Alive

up the grave and prove that he is not there. Hell, you can bribe the coroner to say that the body isn't there, or better yet, you can get the coroner to say that drugs were the reason he died so his death can be ruled a suicide. Then Mr. Doyle, the estate will have to pay all the royalties back to you and to DELTA Records. Then you will have the money to pay me what you owe me."

"Mr. Enricci, we cannot dig up the grave of Elvis Presley!" Governor Chambers' voice quivered and shook as he continued.

"I am begging you. You've got to give Winston more time to get your family paid back! The public will not stand for having the remains of Elvis Presley dug up! It just won't work."

Giorgio Enricci walked around the room. He occupied the penthouse at one of Las Vegas' most beautiful casino resorts. He went to the bar next to a large picture window and poured himself a straight Scotch. He then walked back to face the silver-haired politician and the tall, trembling CEO of DELTA Records. He walked past Rex Chambers and put his pudgy hand around the back of Winston Doyle's neck.

"You better tell your good friend, the governor, to follow the advice of our legal counsel. You really have no recourse. As CEO of DELTA records you've squandered a fortune. Most of that money belongs to the Enricci family...."

"Son, listen to the advice of Giorgio. You have to talk your friend, the governor, into digging up this Elvis Presley. Whether he is there or not, you will pay off the coroner in Memphis to say that his body is not there. You have no choice in this matter. How else are you going to get hundreds of millions of dollars? Don't listen to this politician. He doesn't have to pay your debt!"

"Listen to Giorgio. This Elvis Presley caused me great pain one time. I, Giorgio, once had a beautiful girl. She was a movie star. She loved me and I loved her. Then this Elvis Presley came to Las Vegas. He did these shows." Giorgio Enricci swept his arm across the breadth of the window. The city of Las Vegas glistened and twinkled below.

"This Elvis," Giorgio furrowed his brow and continued the sweeping of his arm, obviously becoming agitated, "this Presley," he spat, "he came wiggling into town and stole her love from Giorgio!"

"He did not love her, not like an Enricci could. Not like I, Giorgio, would! I could have made her into a big star. But this Elvis!" he screamed at the top of his lungs, shimmering and shaking his fat backside in mockery. After his rage had subsided, the small, fat Sicilian turned to both men. "Now you both owe me a great deal of money! I want to have a small favor repaid me as well as the money paid me."

He turned to Governor Chambers. "You control that little state. Your people treated the Cherokee Indians there like dogs. Your forefathers passed the law that will allow us to dig this grave up and take the money from his estate. The Enricci family is only taking advantage of the law that your people used to rape another people. You can't change the law now, and you must live by it." Giorgio walked up to Winston Doyle. Winston's tall frame actually shook.

"Let me tell you an old Sicilian tale," Giorgio said. His slicked-back hair glistened as he spoke.

"There was once a young man who wanted to

be very, very rich." He waved his finger again in the air to punctuate the story and his point. "This young man also wanted to be very powerful. He came to the Enricci Godfather and asked to be made rich and powerful: no small request considering he was from such a poor station in life and was of such limited talents.

"The Godfather granted his request, with one stipulation! He would not forget the Godfather and would one day repay him with a small favor." Giorgio waved his whole hand in the air.

"Well, the young man took the favors of the Enricci family and prospered, not by anything that he did, mind you, but by the power of the Godfather!"

Giorgio's face had lost its smile. The veins on his neck began to bulge. His temples pounded with anger.

"When the Godfather asked many years later for a favor in return—not a large favor, mind you, but a small favor like I'm asking you now—well, the young man forgot his promise. He ignored the request of my family." Giorgio was shouting now. For a short, fat man, he sure could scream. The windows of the penthouse shook with the high pitch of his voice.

"The Godfather had one of the family members to go to the young man and plead with him to remember the promise he had made years earlier. The young man acted as if he had never heard of the Enricci Godfather." Suddenly, Giorgio Enricci lowered his voice to a normal decibel. A smile returned to his pudgy little face. He ran his hand through his hair, flipping the short ponytail tied at the end. He smiled broadly at Rex Chambers and Winston Doyle.

"The young man later said he wished he had remembered his promise to the Godfather." Giorgio laughed slightly. "He said this right before I cut off his...genitals."

Giorgio smiled. "He said he remembered his promise then, but that was all he said, because I stuffed his genitals in his mouth and then I disemboweled him, and a few minutes later he was dead."

Giorgio crossed his short arms. He looked at Winston with his arms still crossed and his head tilted back on his neck as far as it would go. His beady little eyes glowered at Winston.

"Son, you can do whatever you want, but let me give you some advice. If you want to live, you will do what I and my family's lawyers tell you to do or...you will wind up like the unfortunate young man in my story."

Winston Doyle trembled even more. He looked around like a doe with bright headlights focused on it. He looked at Governor Chambers. Winston walked over the marble floor to Rex.

"You've got to help me," he sobbed and pleaded. "You've got to help me do what Giorgio says. I don't want to die!" He tumbled to the floor. Large tears welled up in his eyes They spilled onto the marble, creating a small puddle in seconds. He got on his knees and pulled at Rex Chambers' trousers.

"Please, please, Rex," he looked up with reddened eyes. "Help me get the state of Tennessee to dig him up! I'll do anything for you politically that I can. You and I both owe Giorgio!" He broke down in big, deep sobs.

"Rex, I've blown all that money. I can't get

anymore. Giorgio's way is the only way. Trust me. We'll use that Cherokee law to dig him up. The man is dead, what difference will it make?"

Winston Doyle writhed on the floor sobbing. Finally, Governor Rex Chambers pulled the distraught man up from the marble floor.

"Okay, okay, we'll do it," he said. "But let me tell you that I'm against this. You guys don't know what kind of craziness this is going to unleash. It will be horrible."

Giorgio slapped his hands together and rubbed them happily. "That's the spirit, bambinos!" He walked over and put his arms around the two men.

"You will never regret this. You've made the right decision. I'll get my lawyers to help you both whenever you're ready to get started."

Winston Doyle jumped around. "Absolutely, Giorgio." He turned to Chambers and said, "Rex, we'll get to work on this right—"

"I don't see that we have much of a choice in the matter," Chambers interrupted.

"Good boys," the fat Sicilian congratulated them. Turning back to the window he repeated, "Good boys. I knew you two would see it my way." He laughed a curious high-pitched laugh and slapped his hands together again as if he were sitting down to a delicious meal. He laughed again, then spat out, "Looks like ole Giorgio is going to have everything he used to own. I guess I'll even own that shack in Memphis where he's buried." Giorgio continued to laugh and slapped his little hands together once more.

"I never liked that swivel-hipped son of a bitch."

* * * * *

The Orient Express rounded another curve. The whistle sounded again from above. I looked over at Elvis. His eyes were closed tightly. His jaw was clenched and a frown of consternation was etched over his face.

I knew that parts of this story would upset him. I had been reluctant from the first to tell him everything. How could the story be told with only half the truth out there? It wouldn't make any sense. Besides, if he didn't want to hear anymore, he could get up and leave. I must admit I was still a bit star-struck. Just because I was a friend now hadn't diminished the fact that I was a big fan. And it didn't change the fact that finding him was a miracle!

Still I felt somewhat guilty for upsetting him. He was my friend and it's always upsetting to hurt your friends.

Elvis slowly opened his eyes. His teeth were still gritted together. He turned to me slowly, moving his head only. Looking at me, he smiled.

"I knew a lot of this would be upsetting," he said, his dark skin fairly glistening.

"You know, I never drink, but right now I could use a drink."

I looked at him in disbelief.

"I can't believe it. Elvis Presley is going to drink some whiskey!"

Elvis smiled. "I'll probably just sip on it. Come on, let's go to the sitting car. We need a break from this location anyway."

We got up and headed out into the hall of the swaying car. Elvis looked back over his shoulder with disgust.

"Did you know that I knew that skunk, Rex

Chambers?"

I shook my head negatively.

"Yeah, I knew him way back then, and he called me a friend."

"Elvis, with friends like Rex Chambers, as the old saying goes...." Then we both said in unison, "Who needs enemies!"

"You know, Dr. St. John," he added. "I knew that Enricci guy, actually not that well. I just wish I knew which girl he was talking about!"

Chapter Fourteen

The sitting car was packed with people. The smoke was as thick as a London fog. The different aromas were marvelous. In France, people are still allowed to smoke in public.

We sat down next to an older couple. He was smoking a burl wood pipe. She had gray hair and was smoking a strong French cigarette. I knew they were aware of us as soon as we sat down. I didn't know what was on their minds, but I could sense they were talking about us.

When the waitress came by, we both ordered Jack Daniel's. It was my favorite drink, and Elvis said he would sip on it and look sophisticated.

"Young man," the older woman tapped Elvis on his shoulder.

"Yes ma'am," he replied in his constant polite and well-mannered tone.

"Excuse me for saying this, but you look exactly like Elvis Presley. I bet you're told that all the time, aren't you?"

"Yes ma'am, I am told that all the time, since I work as an Elvis impersonator. I perform at the Elvis Review in Paris." He reached in his pocket and pulled out a business card and handed it to her." Here, I would like it if you both would come and see me perform sometime."

She took the card gratefully and showed it to her husband. "See, Harry, I told you it was something like that. Presley has been dead forever," she said self-knowingly.

"Thank you, young man." She smiled at Elvis. "If we have time, we'll come to see you in Paris." She turned around to enjoy her smoke with Harry.

Elvis winked at me and whispered, "See, it works every time."

The waitress brought us our drinks. I drank mine with gusto. Elvis, true to his word, sipped gingerly. I doubt that he actually drank any of it. He did comment on the special flavor and the cool burn it imparted on his lips. I think we both had ordered it out of Tennessee state pride.

"Do you miss Graceland?" I blurted out, my blushing face betraying my embarrassment, I had momentarily forgotten our agreement that I would tell my story first, but my embarrassment was more in the personal nature of my question. It was the first question I had asked that was so close to his private life. I also was uncomfortable with the fact that I had asked him in front of so many people, although I doubt anyone was paying attention to me.

"I miss it horribly," he responded without as much as a flinch. He brought the amber fluid back to his lips and let its sting linger on his pursed lips for what seemed like forever.

"Yes, I ache for my Graceland," he whispered, never looking at me. His sad countenance made me regret my curiosity. Why couldn't I have held my tongue? He would have gotten into his personal feelings later.

"I'm sorry," I began.

He interrupted, "Don't worry. I'm fine. I still want to tell you everything. It'll just be hard, that's all." He looked at me with a sad smile. "Why don't you go ahead with your story. It's going to be a very interesting adventure, I can tell." The sadness suddenly left his face and he smiled. Lifting his glass, he said,

"I propose a toast. A toast to Dr. St. John and the adventure that led him to find me and gave us an opportunity to become friends."

"Hear, hear," I saluted back. We clinked glasses. I took a giant drink, and he pretended to drink his.

"Let's go back to the room. We have so much to discuss," Elvis said, looking around at the people in the car.

We got up and walked through the sitting car. The smoke that had clouded the air followed us, at least on our clothing. Some of that smoke was strong: My eyes actually burned.

As soon as we returned to our car he turned to me and asked, "What more can you tell me about that snake, the governor?"

"Well, let's see," I responded as I sank down into the seat, getting comfortable. I thought back, trying to remember all the events leading to my search. Some of them were disjointed and seemingly nonrelated, but as with any jigsaw puzzle, when you put the pieces together a clear picture emerges.

"Let me go back to Memphis. I'll tell you about the night I went home and talked with Marcia after my first meeting with Governor Chambers and Dr. Regent."

"Yeah, tell me all of that stuff. Don't get too far

ahead of yourself. I want to know all the events that led you on this long sojourn, as Babette would say."

* * * * *

After leaving the administrator's office, I wandered around for a long time. I went by the ER on the off chance that Marcia had waltzed in. The chaos that went with the Emergency Room tumbled all around me, but no Marcia. I decided I needed a drink. I didn't really understand the full implications of all that had transpired that day. Little did I know that my meeting with Governor Chambers and Dr. Regent would change my life forever.

It's strange how a single event can totally redirect one's life, but it can, especially if you're not privy to all that is going on around you. The thing many people don't realize, and I didn't for a long time, is how a single episode in your mind can be so interrelated to others.

After I left the ER, I decided to go over to Overton Square and have a drink. A lot of people from the hospital went to TGI Friday's, which is on the corner of the square, to have a drink after work. I hoped I would see someone I knew. As far as I was concerned, I could tell everyone about this. What difference would it make? I had no idea the wild scenario that had unfolded in front of me in Dr. Regent's office would ever come to pass.

I needed a drink. I also needed to talk to someone.

"Dr. St. John, Dr. St. John, I'm over here." The voice of Dr. Bickley Cross drifted from across the corner of the bar. Her hand was waving from a corner table. Great, now I had someone to talk to, a confidante. We exchanged small talk. She wanted to know how her compatriot, Marcia, was doing.

"Okay, I guess. I haven't seen her today."

"What are you having to drink?" Bickley asked.

"The usual, Jack Daniel's on the rocks."

"That's what all you Tennesseans drink!"

"It's Tennessee Tea, Bickley."

Bickley was from Washington, D.C. She didn't really seem to understand people from the deep South, but she seemed to tolerate us.

When the waitress came by, I ordered my Jack, and Bickley ordered a Miller Lite. The light beer she drank didn't help her figure any. She was a short, squat woman, but her face was sort of pretty. She continually pulled her short brown hair back, and her eyeglasses didn't accentuate her eyes, but she didn't seem to care much about her appearance. Bickley was one of those people who seemed to care only about her job as an ER doctor. She was always friendly and enthusiastic. I asked about the ER and then she asked me about the coroner's office. It was just the opening I needed.

"Bickley, let me tell you what happened today." I was interrupted by the waitress bringing our drinks to the table. Before I could continue, Bickley looked over at the door. She threw up her hand and waved wildly. "Marcia, I'm over here trying to steal your man."

Marcia smiled and walked over to greet us.

She kissed me and said, "I knew I couldn't trust you two," as she sat down between us.

She and Bickley immediately began to discuss recent interesting cases they had seen in the Emergency Department. Ironically, back in the early eighties, the main trauma center where they worked had been renamed the Elvis Presley Trauma Center.

As the conversation wound down, I blurted out, "They're trying to dig up your main benefactor." I knew they had heard me because they looked at me and smiled. They seemed to not understand or believe me and just ignored my comment.

"They're trying to dig up Elvis Presley!" I whispered above their conversation, leaning forward in my chair to get their attention. They continued to talk, ignoring me as women will do when they are deep in conversation.

I took a deep gulp of my Jack Daniel's. I knew I had an incredible story to tell if only I could get their attention.

Elvis interrupted my train of thought. "Women are like that sometimes, aren't they?"

"Yes, they are," I agreed.

The Orient Express continued to barrel down the tracks. I looked outside. It had become dark. I hadn't noticed because I was so intent on telling an interesting story.

Elvis looked a little sheepish.

"Sorry, I didn't mean to interrupt you. Go ahead and tell me what happened. How did you finally get their attention?"

"You know, I just kept talking and they finally listened." The whistle blew again, signaling the approach of a road crossing. I continued the story where I had left off.

"Yeah, the governor and I are going to be really close if this thing goes through." Finally Marcia looked at me questioningly.

"Robert, what are you talking about? Bickley and I are discussing an interesting abruptio placenta that came into the ER yesterday."

I just batted my eyes nonchalantly. "Oh, I'm sure that's interesting, but I don't think it's nearly as interesting as what Governor Rex Chambers told me in Dr. Regent's office today." That finally got their attention.

Simultaneously they both exploded, "The governor?"

"What does he want with you?" Marcia asked.

"Oh, nothing really. He just wants me to be aware that there's a lawsuit brewing that might involve me and the coroner's office." That really got their attention.

"What lawsuit? What are you talking about?" I decided to be coy, to pay them back for their earlier inattention.

"I don't know if I really should discuss this with you two. After all, you weren't at the meeting. I don't know if the governor and Dr. Regent would want me to discuss this with just anybody."

Marcia hit me firmly but playfully across the shoulder and then brushed the hair that her "blow" had caused to fall down over my forehead.

"Robert, if you don't tell me..." she sputtered. I simply smiled. "You won't believe this story."

"Tell us, tell us!" They were both leaning forward, goading me on.

"I was in Dr. Regent's office today. He told me the most bizarre story you can imagine." I had finished my drink and took my time in motioning for the waitress.

"Go on, go on!" they exhorted. I definitely had their attention now. I waited for the waitress to refill my drink before I continued.

Marcia shook me by the shoulder.

"Hurry up and tell us," she demanded.

"Well," I finally started again, "it seems as if Priscilla Presley has asked the governor to intercede on her behalf to prevent DELTA Records from exhuming the body of the late Elvis Presley." I tried to be as nonchalant as I could as I explained this to them.

"NO WAY!" they both shouted at once.

"Oh yes!" I answered. "Dr. Regent introduced me to the governor in his office just an hour or so ago."

"What did Governor Chambers want exactly?" Marcia asked incredulously.

"He wanted to get to know me. As coroner for Shelby County and Memphis, I'll be required to supervise the exhumation of the body." I admit I laughed at that proposition, it was so outrageous.

Bickley and Marcia looked at each other. They then turned their gaze to me as if I were nuts.

I took another drink of Jack and smiled at them. "I know, I know how crazy it seems."

I still had a big smile on my face, not necessarily from the story I was telling them but from the attention I was getting.

"But the fact remains that Governor Rex Chambers met with me and said he wanted me to be prepared for anything that might happen."

"But why?" Marcia finally asked the big question.

"Marcia, I'm not really sure. It has something to do with royalties.... It seems the record company wants money back from the Presley estate. But listen to this! There's actually a law on the books that allows them to exhume the body if there is a question about the circumstances of his death."

"You mean those nuts that believe Elvis is still alive?" Bickley adjusted her glasses as she did often when she was thinking.

"I guess so, Bickley. Isn't this weird? It's like something out of a crazy novel or something!"

Bickley and Marcia agreed with a nod of their heads.

"So let me get this straight." Marcia exhaled deeply and began to lean forward to me as she spoke.

"Some record company wants to get back the royalty money they've paid the Presley estate because a bunch of nuts have said they've seen Elvis alive."

"That's the way I understand it. I know it sounds crazy, but that's the way Governor Chambers explained it to me."

"Life *is* stranger than fiction," Bickley exclaimed as she gave out a "Dada dada, dada dada" mimicking the Twilight Zone theme.

"What next then?" Marcia asked.

"I don't know for sure."

"Surely this won't happen, Robert." Marcia was adamant in her disbelief.

"Yeah, it's impossible," Bickley agreed. "This is crazy. How would they go about it?"

"Ooh, I don't think it's really going to happen either. Dig up Elvis Presley? Who do they think they are kidding." I took another swig of Jack Daniel's.

"Can you imagine the furor that would create?" I smiled at the two young women.

"Hell, it would probably cause a riot."

Bickley took a drink of Miller Lite, wiped her mouth and agreed, "Yeah, riot is probably not even the right word. It would be an international scandal, a circus. I just can't imagine something like this coming off. Surely they'll come to an agreement or something."

"Yeah," Marcia agreed. "The man has been dead for almost twenty years, and his fans are still the most loyal in the world. I can't imagine them letting something like this happen. No, it's impossible. Something like this could never happen in this country."

Marcia's point was well taken. We agreed with her by shaking our heads in acknowledgment.

With that we all quieted down and concentrated on our drinks, but the silence was an uneasy one. For some reason, whether it was the governor's visit or the sheer absurdity of the situation, we all felt a disquieting cloud hovering over us.

Not much more was said. Bickley had another Miller Lite. I had one more Jack Daniel's. Marcia had a Coca-Cola. For some reason I regretted bringing the subject up. It could have been a lively source of conversation; instead, it put us in a foul mood.

A few minutes later, Marcia and I decided to go home. Bickley said she was going to have another beer and then go home herself.

"Keep me posted," Bickley demanded as we were leaving.

"I will," I promised.

Our apartment was in Midtown, not far from Friday's. It took only a few minutes to walk there. Marcia and I continued to be in somber moods as we made our way home.

After we entered our apartment, Marcia turned

to me with pleading eyes and said, "This is going to happen, isn't it, Robert? It makes me sad somehow. I hope you'll have no part in it because it would be just plain wrong."

I pulled her close to me, hugging her in a reassuring manner. "No way will this happen, Marcia. I think the governor is panicking." I tried to be persuasive, but I think the doubt in my voice spilled out.

"No, no way is this going to happen."

I tried to be more positive and self-assured as I began to kiss her neck. "Let's forget that I even brought the subject up. It's too damn morbid. Let's do something to get our minds off this," I said as I pulled her into the bedroom.

"You wicked little boy," she teased. "Was this whole story just a ploy to get me into bed?" With that we both laughed and fell into bed.

* * * * *

It had become jet black outside the train. We could make out distant lights, which I assumed to be isolated farmhouses. After I had finished that part of the story I looked up at Elvis. His eyes were still closed, but there was no emotion displayed on his face. He finally responded by saying,

"It's an interesting story, but it's getting late. Why don't we get some shuteye. You can pick up the story tomorrow. I'm real interested to see where this is going to go."

"So you're not offended then?"

He simply shrugged, "If I ever want you to quit, I'll tell you. Don't worry. Besides Dr. St. John, this helps me...in some strange way. And I look forward to telling you some things."

He didn't know how much I wanted to hear them, but I kept that thought as hidden as I could.

"You know, Dr. St. John, you're the first person—other than Babette I guess—that I've allowed to get close to me since I changed...my life. I guess that's the way to describe it."

"Elvis," I began to interrupt.

He held up his hand as a sign for me to listen. "Alfonso's death had more of an impact on me than you might imagine. I'm looking forward to confiding in someone. It's something I never thought I would want to do after all these years, but it will be a burden lifted in a way. Let's get some sleep. We'll continue in the morning."

We got into the separate pull-out beds that were cleverly hidden in the car. The darkness outside was broken by the light of the stars and occasional farmhouses. The train clattered on down the track, oblivious to the lives of the people it carried. I tried to imagine all of the people who had shared this room before us. It would have been an interesting history, I'm sure.

I was almost asleep when Elvis asked me, "Did you read the article in the *London Globe* that told about how MY ghost was trying to contact Princess Di?"

"No," I laughed. "I can't say I've heard about that one."

"Yeah, it's wild," he said as he rolled over to go to sleep. "Doc, you can't possibly imagine what it's like to be Elvis Presley."

Robert Mickey Maughon, M.D.

Chapter Fifteen

I was awakened by the sun shining on my face. I must have slept hard. I don't remember stirring once during the night. I looked over at Elvis in the next bunk and decided not to disturb him. Instead I would go on and get some breakfast in the dining car by myself. I imagined he was exhausted from the way he continued to snore as I was dressing. I slipped out of the car, being careful not to awaken him as I headed to the dining car. There was a large crowd already assembled for breakfast.

The one lone seat available was at a side corner table. I sat down and ordered a cup of coffee; the exotic brand that Elvis had introduced to me and that I enjoyed so much.

We had passed Verona and were headed north to Austria. The countryside had become greener. We stopped at some stations long enough for the passengers to get off and do a little sightseeing, but right now all I cared about was having more private time with Elvis. I sensed he was gaining a lot of interest in my story.

"Excuse us, we met you at from the Elvis Review in Paris. You're from Tennessee, aren't you?"

It was Albert and Phyllis, the couple from Oregon who had sat near me at the theater.

"Hey, we saw you get on the train with the Elvis impersonator," Phyllis said.

"Are you guys friends?"

"No, we're just acquaintances."

"He looks just like Elvis, don't you think?" she asked.

I smiled at them, trying to speak as little as possible. These people were nice enough, but I had no desire to spend all morning with them. I took my coffee and headed back to our car.

"See you later," Phyllis called out after me.

I waved with my free hand, taking care not to spill my coffee. I had to negotiate past a couple of more people in the narrow hall as I headed back to the room. I carefully opened the door, thinking Elvis would still be asleep.

I was wrong. He was up shaving.

"Hey Dr. St. John, I see you're an early bird."

"Do you mind ordering me some coffee while I shave?"

"Certainly. What do you want?"

"The same, Doc. Yours certainly smells good!"

I had no more than ordered when the waiter appeared with a pot full of hot java. I poured Elvis a cup.

"Thanks. That's great," he said, as he took a deep sip.

"We're going to be stopping in Austria soon. Would you like to get off and see the sights or are you anxious to get back to Paris?"

I shrugged my shoulders. "It doesn't matter to me. Whatever you want to do."

He had just finished shaving when he walked

Robert Mickey Maughon, M.D.

over and sat down on the chair opposite me.

"Well, while we're making up our minds, do you mind taking up where you left off last night? I know this story is about me, and it's uncomfortable at times to hear, but I have to admit that it's a good story."

"Of course I don't mind. That's why I'm here, remember?"

He smiled even more and spread his hands out in front of him as if to say, "What are you waiting for then?"

I took a big sip out of my white porcelain cup and began telling my adventure again.

* * * * *

The next two weeks after my meeting with Governor Chambers and Dr. Regent were quiet. As I didn't really expect to hear anything from Dr. Regent, or the governor for that matter, I went about my job, minding my own business. I had learned from my conversation with Bickley and Marcia that the subject of exhuming Elvis Presley's body was one that was definitely a downer. Since I thought the point was moot, I decided not to tell anyone else about it. Marcia and I were living our normal solid little lives. I went to work. She went to work. I performed autopsies. She saved lives in the ER.

I was totally unprepared for the call I received from Dr. Regent that July day. Mrs. Mason, his secretary, called and left a message at the apartment that said Dr. Regent wanted to see me at his office when I had a chance.

It was time for my biannual job performance

review, so I didn't really think much about it. As I had a busy schedule that week, I decided to go by his office when I had time that Friday.

Dr. Regent is a pretty laid-back type of guy, but when I rounded the hall to his office, I could hear him yelling at Mrs. Mason from the door that opened into his office. I couldn't make out much of what he was saying, but I could hear some profanity.

As soon as he saw me at the door, he ushered Mrs. Mason out of his office.

"Well, they've done it," he exploded.

"Done what?" I asked, trying to remain composed.

"You've got to go to Nashville."

"Nashville? What for?" I asked, obviously confused.

"To meet with some lawyers for a deposition."

I sat down in the big chair I had occupied when I had first interviewed for the coroner's job. "What for, some kind of murder case?"

"No, no. Don't you remember Governor Chambers' being here two weeks ago and telling you that you may have to exhume Elvis?"

I didn't know how to respond. I think I sat there with my mouth open before I managed to say, "You're kidding me!"

"No, my young friend. That idiot Winston Doyle is trying to prove that Elvis killed himself with drugs—a suicide, in their opinion, or hell, that he isn't dead! They say too many people will testify to seeing him alive for him to possibly be dead. Of course all they care about is this damn money dispute. They don't care about the family or the fans. They just want their money back."

"Why, then, do I have to go to Nashville?"

"You have to explain about the accuracy of a new coroner's report after the body has been buried all of these years."

"Why me?"

"Because you're the coroner here. You'll be the one exhuming the body and doing the postmortem if these idiots get their way."

I looked at Dr. Regent in disbelief. I had thought all of this was kind of funny at first. Now that I was suddenly confronted with the possibility of performing this grisly task, I was in shock. No, shock was not strong enough a word. I don't know how to accurately describe the numb feeling I felt.

"When do I have to go?"

"Next week. You need to meet with lawyers from both sides of the case, I guess. I'm not sure about the details. This is out of the blue for me too. I just know they're trying to keep it top secret."

Dr. Regent crooked two fingers on both of his hands in front of him as if to place "top secret" in quotes.

"You can imagine what the press would do with this!"

I don't remember leaving Dr. Regent's office or seeing or talking to Mrs. Mason. I just wanted to get home and to talk to Marcia.

I sure as hell didn't want to dig up Elvis Presley. And I didn't want to go to Nashville to give statements to lawyers. Why did they need me? What would I tell them...that the odds of learning anything from any kind of examination at this time would most certainly be useless.

This situation was purely about money and had to be political or else some kind of personal vendetta. I walked in a fog that was my current state of consciousness to the apartment. This has to be a bad dream or a nightmare, or at least I hoped it was!

Marcia wasn't there. I never drink during the day except on special occasions. I considered this special. As we didn't keep any alcoholic beverages in the house, I walked down to the corner liquor store.

Leon, who sometimes acted as a night watchman at the apartment, was behind the counter at the store. He knew something was wrong immediately.

"Dr. St. John, you look like you've seen a ghost!"

"Leon, maybe I have, or maybe I will."

"Why don't you get something to drink then."

"Buddy, that's the reason I'm here. Have you got any Jack Daniel's, Black Label?"

Leon gave me the biggest bottle on the counter and I paid him. He advised me to go home and take a drink.

"No make that two," Leon said as I left. "You're white as a sheet!"

"I will, Leon. I'll go do that right now."

The walk back to the apartment was less traumatic than the one from work. I wanted no part of the scenario that Dr. Regent was talking about. The more I thought about it, the more preposterous it became. Imagine, the thought of going into Graceland and exhuming the body of a man who had been dead for almost twenty years.

"They wouldn't do that," I declared out loud as I walked into the front door of the apartment.

"Who wouldn't do what?" the startled voice of Marcia came from the kitchen.

"Thank God you're here!" I exclaimed as I ran into the kitchen. I broke out the bottle, poured a full glass and took a deep gulp in front of an astonished Marcia.

"You never drink at home! What were you talking about?"

A puzzled look played across her face. It turned into a look of worry as I took another large drink.

"Do you remember the story I told you and Bickley at Friday's a couple of weeks ago?"

"The thing about digging up the body of Elvis Presley and all of that crazy stuff?"

"Yeah, well, guess what? I'm going to Nashville next week to talk to lawyers about doing just that!"

I poured another large drink.

Marcia looked at me with large eyes. I'm sure she was surprised not only by my statement but by the size of the drink I was consuming. It was totally out of character.

"What in the world do they want you to tell them?" Marcia's look of worry had turned to a look of incredulity.

"Who is doing this and what do they think they will learn from you?"

"It's like I said in the bar, Winston Doyle of DELTA Records is behind this. They think I am going to tell them what we can learn from an autopsy of a man who has been dead for twenty years." I took another large drink.

"I can't believe this is happening," she said.

"This is the dumbest thing I've ever heard of. How do they think they're going to get away with this?"

"I don't know Marcia. I don't want to have anything to do with it. Can you understand my

Elvis Is Alive

feelings? I think it is morally wrong for the state to do something like this."

"Oh Lord, yes, Robert, I agree one hundred percent with you that this is wrong as well as being nutty. What will you do?"

"I don't think I have any choice. I'll have to go to Nashville and try to give these record company people a piece of my mind. I'll tell them that virtually nothing can be learned from a situation like this."

Marcia came up and hugged me around the neck.

"I'm sorry that you're involved in this. Can you imagine how the Presley family must feel?"

That weekend passed slowly. I kept playing over and over in my mind what I would say: this plan was ridiculous and I could see nothing positive being gained from this action.

Little did I know at the time that I was just a cog in a wheel of action that had already been set in motion, and like the great earth itself, it could not be stopped by anyone other than God.

Sometimes events in life are like that, unstoppable once the actions are set in motion. I did not know Giorgio Enricci. I didn't know the vendetta he held against Elvis. I didn't know about the hold he had over Winston Doyle, or over Governor Rex Chambers. I thought these two men were simply stupid or evil. It wasn't until much later that I found out that they were cowards and that their cowardice had allowed this travesty to occur.

I would learn not to be so gullible and naive in the future. When I went to Nashville that week, I thought our honorable governor was acting out of loyalty to the law, that he had no other choice than to enforce that law. Winston Doyle was just a big wimp. In Nashville, I thought he was looking after the bottom line of his company. Both of them should have been strung up from the nearest tree. No one would know the truth about them and about Giorgio Enricci until it was too late.

* * * * *

The train slowed down as we approached a station. As we came to a stop, Elvis said, "Let's order a bite to eat. We can talk more as we eat." He then shook his head and said, "Boy, I didn't know that all of this went on."

"Don't worry, Elvis, it gets better."

We ordered sandwiches and made small talk.

"So, what happened in Nashville?" Elvis asked, not looking up from of his sandwich.

"Well, your ex, Priscilla, also went to Nashville and gave the group assembled there a piece of her mind!"

Elvis gave me a funny look. "Priscilla?"

"Oh yeah! That woman has spunk and character. She was a sight to behold! No one is going to take advantage of her...especially if it means hurting Lisa Marie!"

"Go ahead," he motioned with his sandwich in his hand excitedly. "Tell me what happened."

Chapter Sixteen

I started to recall that day. It was a time I'll never forget as long as I live. I left for Nashville on a drizzly Thursday. It was kind of unusual weather for July in Tennessee. I drove my Jaguar XKE up Interstate 40 in sort of a daze. Tennessee is such a long state that I had plenty of time to reflect on my way.

I went over and over in my head what I was going to say and how I was going to act. I wished Marcia could have come with me, but she couldn't leave work. I had thought Dr. Regent would go with me, but he declined. He said he would be at the hearing if it was necessary. Like me, he thought this preposterous situation would dry up and blow away if it was opened up to a little scrutiny.

"I'll be in court if it ever makes it that far my boy!" were his reassuring last words in Memphis as I left for Music City, USA.

I had decided to go by Governor Chambers' office first. I didn't really know where else to go. All I had been told was that I was going to explain to the representatives of DELTA Records and the Presley family the nature of a latent autopsy and what it will reveal.

I knew a little about Nashville, but not much.

Robert Mickey Maughon, M.D.

I had gone to the Grand Ole Opry once as a child. I had been to a couple of Tennessee–Vanderbilt football games, which UT won, of course. On this rainy day those kinds of events were the farthest thing from my mind. I wanted to swoop in, answer the questions asked of me and hurry home.

I was able to find the Capitol building fairly easily. Downtown Nashville is easy to drive through. The old statehouse is beautiful in the classical Greek style, as is Nashville's replica of the Parthenon in Centennial Park.

I parked at the old Hermitage Hotel, just a few blocks away. I took an umbrella that Marcia had given me and trudged up the hill to the Capitol, where I crossed the large marbled foyer and walked across the floor to the governor's office. My footsteps echoed throughout the hall as I approached the closed door. The building was strangely quiet. I had expected a constant hubbub from state senators and lobbyists as they discussed legislation.

"You idiots," came the loud female voice from behind the governor's closed door. I could hear the anger in her voice even though I was twenty yards away.

"What you are doing is blasphemy! I will sue the state of Tennessee for everything that every citizen in the state owns if you go through with this nonsense!"

I hesitated as I reached the office. I didn't want to enter, but I felt compelled to go in. It seemed crazy, but I felt as if I was supposed to be there to help the lady who was yelling so angrily. Right before I pushed through the door, I heard Rex Chambers' voice, "Now, now, dear. I think I can explain."

Elvis Is Alive

I opened the door without knocking and walked in.

"What the hell do you want?" Governor Chambers growled until he saw my face and recognized me.

"Oh come in, Dr. St. John!" His voice turned very friendly. The lady who had apparently been doing all of the yelling had her back to me.

"This is the doctor who will supervise the exhumation of the…er…hm," the politician searched for a euphemism, "the body at Graceland." With that accomplished, he smiled weakly and walked to me with an extended open hand.

I had never seen the governor so rattled. The calm exterior was gone. He was as gray as a ghost. I imagined that his hand trembled a bit as I shook his. And his palm was soaking wet! I didn't have time to say anything.

The lady whirled around. I stood face to face with Priscilla Presley.

I was dumbfounded, totally at a loss for words. I must have looked like a fool with my mouth hanging open. I'm not sure, but I think I said, "Hello, Ms. The King…I mean Ms. Priscilla …er…Ma. Presley." And like a fool, I did a half-curtsy, half-bow as if she were Queen Elizabeth.

"Idiots!" she yelled and slapped me so hard I was knocked against the wall.

"I should have known there would be some bloodsucking doctor involved in this!" Her face, though beautiful, was contorted in anguish and anger.

I wanted to explain. I tried to tell her that I was here to derail this mockery before it could go any further, but I couldn't. The words wouldn't come out.

Priscilla stormed past me. Before she left she turned to us both. The color had drained from her face.

"Don't you fellows think you can do this and get away with it," she hissed.

"When you do this, you don't do this to just Elvis and Priscilla. You do it to his fans. But mostly you do it to...Lisa Marie Presley!"

"And boys," she looked at me and then the governor, "there...is...going to be a big price to pay."

She stormed out, slamming the door behind her.

* * * * *

Elvis' laughter caused me to stop in mid-sentence. His usual laugh was more subdued than a classic belly laugh, but he was laughing loudly now. I had never seen him laugh this freely ever before, and I soon found myself joining him.

"Dr. St. John, you caught the wrath of Priscilla Beaulieu Presley full force, didn't you?" He had trouble getting the whole sentence out as he held his side.

"Yeah, I suppose I did," I managed to say as I chuckled at the memory.

"Oh, I'm not laughing at you, Doc," he continued as he noticed some of my embarrassment. "Buddy, let me assure you this old Mississippi boy has been on the receiving end of that wrath. Yes sir, ole Elvis sure as hell caught some of that himself."

I had obviously made him remember some personal moments from his life long ago. He looked at me with a big smile. I was glad I had made him remember something he truly enjoyed reminiscing. It was one of the first times that I didn't feel a twinge of guilt talking about his past life. After all, if a man like Elvis leaves a life like the one he had, one can assume that he wanted to escape some memories, or at least that's what I had conjectured.

He looked at me with a half smirk on his face, still laughing. "Go on, this is becoming interesting."

"Elvis, I can still feel that slap!" I said. We both laughed and I continued the story where I had left off.

* * * * *

The governor and I stared at each other.

"Dr. St. John, am I ever glad you showed up!" he said. Some color began to return to his face.

I rubbed my still-stinging face. "Look, Governor, you're on your own. I'm with the lady. This is nuts!"

He walked over to me and put his hand on my shoulder reassuringly. "Son, let's go into my private office over here and discuss this." He pushed me into his office before I could offer any words of protest.

He closed the big mahogany door behind us to give us some privacy. Soon, Rex Chambers was back to his old political self, smiling and trying to make me feel comfortable. He was a resilient ole bird. Five minutes earlier he had been a meek, beaten-down old man. Now he was charging back, as confident as he could be.

"Dr. St. John, we need to talk. I want you to explain the details of an autopsy like this to a retired judge who will be serving as an arbitrator in a closed and off-the-record trial. Both sides want to try to keep this thing quiet and have agreed to accept the judge's ruling, which will be sealed. If the media got wind of any of this, there's no telling what might happen. It would hurt both sides. No one wants to go through with this thing, but the law is the law. It's very clear in this matter. In a disputed case like this the body will be exhumed, regardless of the time or cause of death, and another autopsy shall be performed." The governor actually seemed to smile to himself.

"I still don't get it," I said, sitting down on his sofa.

Governor Chambers sat down behind his desk. "Dr. St. John, there's a matter of royalties which were paid to an estate over many years and which will be paying many more years in the future. We're talking a huge amount of money. There's also a question of a large insurance payout. When this kind of money is at stake, you can rest assured that the courts will be involved."

"Yeah, but the man has been dead for twenty years, for crying out loud."

"Well, the copyright coverage on songs has been extended by Congress for another fifty years, so we're talking about a huge sum when it comes to an artist like Elvis Presley."

"So it's entirely about money, huh, Governor?"

Governor Chambers got out of his chair and walked to the window overlooking Nashville.

"Yes, Dr. St. John. Isn't that what makes the world go 'round?"

"Does DELTA Records not worry about the repercussions of doing this to a legend...and to his family. I think there will be a price to pay."

Rex Chambers turned to look at me. "Dr. St.

John, I don't know all of Winston Doyle's reasons! As the law reads now—and has read for two hundred years—Elvis Presley's body will be exhumed, and you will be the supervising coroner."

I slumped down in my seat. I was disappointed. I had wanted no part in this, but the governor seemed to know the law. Hell, he was an elected official. If anyone should know the political repercussions of such a stupid act, he would. His attitude seemed to be one of resignation and finality.

I decided then and there that if this event were to occur, I would supervise the exhumation. Before that time I had sworn I would resign before I would participate in such a cowardly act. Now I looked at things differently. If the body was going to be exhumed under these circumstances, I, Robert St. John, M.D., would supervise every detail. I wanted to be able to assure the Presley family that this would be done with as much dignity and class as possible.

I looked up from the sofa. I still had to protest, "But Elvis Presley!"

Governor Chambers never wavered. "The law is the law!"

I sat there stunned and resigned to the circumstances.

"Son, why don't you go get some rest? We'll expect you to be here tomorrow at nine a.m. to testify. Oh, that's not the right word, I mean to talk to the judge." I shook my head in resignation and headed to the door.

The governor stopped me. He appeared more sincere than before.

"Son I know this is hard," he said. "I'm sorry

this task has fallen to you, but if this was just an ordinary case not involving an international celebrity...well, you would be asked to do your duty, wouldn't you?"

I agreed, but it still didn't make the upcoming task any easier. Before I left he stopped me for one last time.

"Dr. St. John, you will probably see Ms. Presley again soon, maybe in the morning. As strong-willed as that woman is, it wouldn't surprise me at all if she put on a similar show at the hearing tomorrow. My point is, don't be too hard on her. After all, she's only protecting what she perceives to be hers and Lisa Marie's."

I rubbed my face. Most of the stinging was gone. "I understand. Governor, I'm on her side!" And with that I shook his hand and left. I walked back across the street to the hotel. Marcia had called and made reservations at the renovated old landmark. I checked in and took the elevator to my room. I walked in and flung myself down on the bed. Again, I began to go over in my mind what I was going to tell the judge tomorrow, I was still going to try to talk him out of ordering this, but I was also resigned to do my duty.

What bothered me most was the secrecy. Winston Doyle and DELTA Records would never do anything like this openly. It would be a public relations nightmare that would make them a target for a boycott of their records and other products. Why were they being allowed to keep their actions secret? If people knew what they were proposing, the public outcry alone would be enough to stop them in their tracks. It didn't make sense.

I was also concerned about my reputation. The

doctor who performed the autopsy would be vilified if word ever got out, and I didn't see how that could be avoided. I knew Elvis' fans would want him whole and undisturbed at Graceland. The thought of me being involved in this charade made me shiver!

Robert Mickey Maughon, M.D.

Chapter Seventeen

I ordered a room-service dinner and settled in to try to get as much rest as I could before the hearing in the morning. It took only a few minutes for me to crawl into bed and try to go to sleep. As I settled under the covers, I took a few moments to reminisce about the crazy happenings of the day.

The thought of Priscilla Presley whopping me on the face made me chuckle—and rub my cheek. I smiled slightly as I drifted off to sleep.

In what seemed like a few minutes I heard: "Good morning, sir, this is your wake-up call. It's seven a.m. Have a nice day!"

"Thank you," I said, rolling over in bed. It took me a moment to realize where I was. I rubbed my eyes. The absurdity of the whole situation made me nauseated.

Splashing water on my face, I stared at myself in the mirror. My reflection bothered me. I worried about doing the right thing. As I shaved, I wondered about my resolve to be the coroner for Memphis. I had a habit of jumping to conclusions or decisions sometimes. I was determined that I was going to put the brake on my decision. As I passed the razor over the side of the face where Priscilla had slapped me the day before, I remembered the commitment I had made to do the right thing as I saw it for the Presley family. I was going to play it by ear. I had felt the wrath of Elvis' ex-wife. I couldn't imagine taking the heat from millions of his fans.

Dressing, I wondered what forces of nature or men were bringing this action. I continued to see no sense in it. I was looking forward to meeting Winston Doyle. Perhaps I could persuade him or his board to back off of their decision. Maybe they could come to a compromise with the Presley estate. As a physician with experience in these matters, I hoped I could explain that they would not gain any knowledge from an autopsy after all these years. An autopsy had been performed right after Elvis died, and no knowledge was gained then. What could they possibly hope to achieve now?

Yes, I would play this by ear. I wanted to be there for the Presley family, to make sure the exhumation would be done with as much dignity as possible. Of course, I was going to fight its being done in the first place. If it became obvious that there was nothing I could do to be of service to the Presley family by being present at exhumation, I would bail out.

I decided to skip breakfast. The nauseated feeling I was experiencing lingered. I hoped that after the hearing was over I would feel like eating lunch.

I walked across the street to the Capitol. I half expected to see a bunch of media trucks out front, but there were none. Everyone involved was doing a good job of keeping the hearing "secret." I covered the granite steps leading up to the building, adjusted my suit and tie, and walked into the eye of the hurricane.

I walked into the governor's office. He wasn't there. "Where is everyone?" I asked one of the governor's secretaries.

"I was supposed to attend a special hearing today."

"That's has been postponed until next Monday."

"Where is Governor Chambers?"

"Search me." She started filing her fingernails.

What in the world is going on here? I wondered. I decided to stay in Nashville that weekend to try to sort things out.

* * * * *

So many times when I was wrapped up in telling the story, I forgot where I was. This happened again when Elvis let out a low unbelieving whistle. I almost jumped through the roof.

"You know, some of this stuff is pretty unbelievable, Dr. St. John."

"You mean you never heard anything about any of it before?"

"I may have seen a tabloid headline about people digging up my grave, but I never knew it might actually be true."

"Would you have surfaced if you had known all of this?" The question slipped out before I could catch myself.

He sighed deeply and looked at me with those dark piercing eyes. "Dr. St. John, I honestly don't know. Tell you what, you tell me the rest of the story, and I'll let you know."

He sighed again. He shook his head in disgust.

"People and money!" was all he said.

He sat with his head hung slightly, staring at the Oriental rug that had been used to cover our Pullman car's floor. I again felt like a heel. I didn't ever want to hurt his feelings. Although none of what happened was my fault, I still felt guilty being the messenger.

When I had been following him, the least of my concerns had been hurting him with this story. Now, this was my uppermost concern.

"Look," I began reluctantly, "if this is too painful for you..." I paused, waiting for a reaction. There was none. He simply looked at that blasted rug.

I continued: "If this is too much, I don't want to say another word."

He interrupted me in a voice so low that at first I didn't know if he was talking or not. "No, it's just—" he stopped short. His eyes dropped and I saw him mouth the words, "Lisa Marie."

Without looking up he began to talk so quietly that I had to lean forward to understand. "No, since Alfonso's death, I've decided to get everything out...no matter how painful."

I've never felt so sorry for a human being in my life. My heart wished it could reach out and comfort his. Then he lifted his head somewhat. He slowly began to smile a little.

His eyes began to twinkle some. All along, since we met in Paris I could tell he admired me for doing something that I'm sure many other people had tried to do, *find him.*

He took some kind of pleasure in the fact that I had promised to tell the story of my trip before he told me his reason for disappearing and faking his own death.

That was fine with me. I'm sure it was a pride thing. After all, I'm positive that he never expected to be sitting with someone like me, someone who had found him, not after all the trouble and effort he had gone through to disappear. I respected that. I shook my head in understanding and laughed.

Whenever I began telling my little adventure, I was amazed at how quickly time flew. I immersed myself in the story so completely that I was shocked every time he interrupted me. Now I looked out the window. I couldn't believe that it was dark again.

"Listen, why don't we knock off for tonight and pick up at the hearing tomorrow," he recommended.

"Good idea."

"We'll be in Switzerland soon. Have you ever seen the Alps?"

"No, I haven't. Are they as pretty as the Smokies or the Rockies?"

Elvis furrowed his brow and thought. "I wouldn't say they're prettier. They're...different."

"Well, I can't wait to see them."

We decided to get ready for bed. I had always felt a little strained being around him before, but not that night. The conversations and experiences we had shared had finally put us at ease.

Also I wasn't as star struck as I had been initially, although occasionally I still had trouble believing that I was having conversations with Elvis Aron Presley I was sharing a train berth with him as if he were my best friend! I was doing okay, considering everything.

Elvis was right about the Alps. They were different! The jagged mountain peaks were the first thing I noticed when I awoke the next morning.

Because the Appalachian chain is the oldest in the world, the mountains have lost a lot of height. The Alps reminded me of the Tetons in their ruggedness. Unlike the Himalayas, on the other hand, they were green.

Elvis noticed me staring at them from my berth.

"I love the mountains," he said. "When I was a kid we would go to the Smoky Mountains. I loved it!"

"I'm from there you know!" I proudly allowed.

He interrupted me. "This may sound perverse, but I can't wait to hear what happened at the trial...or whatever you call it." Now it was his turn to act slightly insecure.

"I insulated myself from the world so completely for so long that I was unaware of how screwy things must have really become."

I laughed a little.

" Well, most of this isn't common knowledge, but you've not even heard the screwy parts yet. Just wait."

He raised his eyebrows a little, and his lip twisted slightly in that famous sneer.

"Let's clean up and get breakfast, and I'll tell you what happened at the hearing," I said.

"I should tell you, though, that the preceding weekend was another hazy one for me. I really wasn't looking forward to testifying at the hearing. I would do my best, but I had to be honest in my assessment of the practicality of performing an autopsy on a man that had been deceased for twenty years."

I looked over at Elvis and said, "Of course, if I

had known that you weren't there, I wouldn't have worried so much." I looked at him with a hint of amusement.

All he did was smile at me.

"What do you want for breakfast?" he asked as he rang for room service.

We ordered bacon and eggs, and I proceeded to tell him about that weekend.

* * * * *

I called Marcia and Dr. Regent. Marcia was scheduled to work through the weekend and couldn't join me, but Dr. Regent told me he would come on Monday. I sat down at my desk at the Hermitage and wrote a short presentation on what could be expected to be found and discerned and what couldn't from a postmortem performed under such circumstances.

I made a notation on how a genetic search of some of Abraham Lincoln's remains had been used to try to discern if he had suffered from Marfan's Syndrome. Marfan's is a genetic condition that causes elongation of the extremities and weakness in certain connective tissues, such as the aorta. In Lincoln's case it was conjectured that the disease might have contributed to mental depression as well. Of course, the latter could not be proved by an autopsy, although the genetic condition possibly could.

I detailed a few of the conditions that could be detected from a postmortem this late. Of course, I'd have to wait for the court hearing to find out what in the world they would be trying to find or achieve with this. I'd be able to address those issues when I found out what they were.

After completing my dissertation, I left the hotel and wandered around downtown Nashville. Second Avenue has been fancied up with a bunch of bars and restaurants. I chose a brew pub. I thought drinking might make me feel better.

At the bar in the pub, I met a lady named Daisy Fillmore from Chattanooga, Tennessee. She was about seventy years old and had come to Nashville by herself to attend a show in the old Ryman Auditorium. Her blue hair belied the youth that still resided in her. She invited me to go with her to see the show, a Patsy Cline review.

* * * * *

"Oh man, I loved Patsy Cline!" Elvis broke in. "I knew her before she was killed in that plane crash." He smiled at me between bites of breakfast.

I looked at him and smiled back. I had forgotten that he would have a soft place in his heart for impersonators, as he was one!

"Anyway," I continued. "We continued to drink beer and chose the house specialty, a wheat-based beer. We finally walked over to the Ryman to see this singer perform as Patsy Cline."

I described the crowds that lined up to see this special performer for Elvis. I thought he would appreciate the different garb everyone wore. There were several people dressed like him!

* * * * *

Before we entered the old, original home of the Grand Ole Opry, Daisy allowed that the show's star was almost as good as Patsy Cline herself. I held my judgment until I had seen her.

The young lady gave a very good rendition of "Crazy" and "Midnight," but I just couldn't give her an unresounding thumbs up. Patsy Cline had a unique voice that couldn't be duplicated!

After the show, I escorted Daisy back to the brew pub. I decided to tell her about what was going to happen on Monday. I instinctively felt I could count on her not to spread the story around.

We sat back at the old oaken bar and drank more of the wheat lager. I explained what was going on, the whole thing as I understood it. She was a great listener and I considered her to be a smart and discreet woman.

"This whole thing is nuts." Her bluish hair bobbed up and down as she tried to be sympathetic after I explained everything.

"There's got to be a lot more going on than you've been told. I think something is rotten in Denmark!"

"Maybe. We'll see," I responded.

"Well, I definitely think you should get a lawyer."

"Daisy, I'm not really a part of this. I'm just a pawn in the process. They're just using me to be thorough or something."

"Still, I think I would have counsel or some kind of legal advice."

I looked at Daisy with consternation.

"I wouldn't know what to ask them or how they would help me. I'm just going to answer questions about the postmortem. I understand that my role is to explain what to expect at an autopsy of someone who has been buried for twenty years."

"Hmm...." Daisy snorted as she took another big drink.

"All the more reason to have an attorney present."

That's how I met William "Red" Shaugnessy.

Chapter Eighteen

A little later, when I returned from a visit to the men's room, Daisy was on the telephone at the end of the bar. I learned in a bit that my ruminations that I *might* talk to an attorney prompted her to call Red. When she explained that he would be up from Chattanooga in a couple of hours, I got a little more than slightly perturbed.

I told her that as a physician, I didn't trust lawyers. I didn't need one for the hearing on Monday. I would be just fine without one. Dr. Regent was going to be with me, and he was the only person I needed!

Daisy looked at me with kind but fierce blue eyes surrounded by that bowl of blue hair that I would later come to see as a halo. I was one put-out doctor as I reluctantly waited at the bar with her for Red. By now it was getting very late. I was hanging around a downtown bar with an old woman I barely knew to meet a lawyer I didn't know and didn't want to know.

Only my Southern upbringing prevented me from storming out the door and heading back to my hotel room at the Hermitage. Surely, if I needed a lawyer I would be provided counsel at the hearing.

"Hmm," Daisy snorted again. "Dr. St. John, with all due respect, you don't know whether you're going to be giving a simple statement, testimony or a deposition....." She shook her blue hair again.

"And you don't even know what they want you to talk about. I advise you to take a drink of beer and wait to talk to Red Shaugnessy!" With that she slammed her mug down and ordered another from the short bartender with the blunted Moe haircut.

* * * * *

"You didn't know this lady at all?" Elvis asked as he was finishing up his breakfast.

"Yeah, I know it sounds crazy, but you had to have been there, Elvis. It was a crazy time. I guess if I hadn't been raised in the South—you know, 'be nice to your elders' and all that."

Elvis laughed. "I understand that. That's just part of being from the South, isn't it?"

"Yeah, I guess so."

We took a few minutes to put out the breakfast dishes and straighten up the room. After we finished, Elvis said, "Tell me about ole Red. He reminds me of someone I knew in Memphis once."

"Ol Red Shaugnessy..." I reminisced, and began to pick up my story.

* * * * *

It was almost midnight before he arrived at the bar in Nashville. He walked in, his thinning red hair flaming. Daisy walked over to the end of the bar and hugged Red around the neck.

"Bartender, get the best lawyer in the world a beer," she said.

Red, Daisy and I sat down together and had a beer. Although I was reluctant to say a lot at first, I eventually told him everything. Everything I knew, that is. It seems strange that I opened up to two basic strangers, but I was feeling pretty lost. Except for my brief exchange with the governor, no one from either side had talked to me about my role in the hearing.

Red Shaugnessy was a good listener. His bushy red eyebrows twitched up and down as I droned on about the meeting with Rex Chambers at Dr. Regent's office in Memphis.

"A crook" was all Red said when I first mentioned the governor's name.

* * * * *

Elvis interrupted me at that point.

"The trip on the Orient Express will be over at noon tomorrow," he said, looking at his watch to emphasize the point.

"Why don't you plan to stay with me in Paris for a few days to finish the story? I have a feeling it's going to get really interesting now."

"You've got the right feeling, buddy, and I'd love to stay with you at the Paris house for a couple of days."

I took my time with the next statement, going slowly so he would not misinterpret what I was saying.

"I can only stay a few days, though. I have to resume my life. I've had a lot of fun." I stretched my hands up to the ceiling of the Pullman car and yawned.

"The girls will probably be there. If not

tomorrow, they'll likely come up from the beach house. I'll call Pierre."

"Well," I hedged.

"Oh, come on, Doc! I'm enjoying your company! Besides, you've got to finish the story."

"Oh, I'm not going anywhere until we finish the whole story! Besides, I've got to get the *whole* story!"

"Hey, a promise is a promise. Don't worry!"

"Okay, Elvis, I'll stay as long as I can."

We didn't discuss Nashville or the hearing again during the rest of the trip into Paris. We spent our time traveling and sightseeing. I was hoping Babette and Brigitte might be at the Paris station when the train arrived. I could tell from Elvis' craned neck he was hoping the same thing. We both anxiously scanned the mass of people who were waiting outside the station.

We had unloaded our luggage and were trying to get it into a taxi when we heard "Robert! Elvis!" The pitched voices of Babette and Brigitte came whistling through the crowd. We turned around and ran to the two vibrant young ladies. There was a lot of hugging and kissing. The girls even shed a few tears.

Elvis told the taxi driver where to take the luggage, and the four of us jumped into the trusty little Peugeot and headed out into the Paris crowds. We had quite a reunion when we arrived at the red brick Paris townhouse.

It was obvious Elvis and Babette were trying to make up. It was also obvious that there was still a lot of friction. What was a man to do? If he still loved Priscilla after all these years, I doubt he would ever get over her.

If he wanted a certain kind of relationship with Babette and she wanted more, well, they would have to work that out. I'm sure it would help Babette understand him if she knew about his former life. It was none of my business. The truth had to come from him. From what I had learned of Elvis, I figured she probably would never know.

They spoke French in staccato, making me wish even more that I knew the language. Traffic kept us in the car for at least an hour. Brigitte and I took up where we had left off. We weren't the ones who had caused all the commotion.

Home! That's what the townhouse felt like as we pulled into the small asphalt driveway that was mostly hidden from the main street. It seemed strange now that a house I had been in only once now felt like home. After spending the last week or so in hotels, I definitely felt as if I had returned home when we reached it.

The place looked bigger in the day. The furniture was plain, as I had noted on my previous visit, but it was tastefully done.

"Pierre!" I heard Elvis saying hello to his loyal houseman.

Sure enough, Pierre was there. He had driven up from the beach with the girls. Everyone rushed to hug the goateed fellow. There was something about Pierre that made everyone like him. Elvis, when excited, called him "Peter." The house was a flurry of activity. Everyone was unpacking and helping Pierre settle into the house.

The first thing Pierre asked was if we were hungry. He waited expectantly for our answer as he cocked his beret rakishly to one side of his head.

"We could eat," Elvis and I spoke simultaneously

and enthusiastically.

Pierre immediately went to the kitchen and began to rummage through the cabinets to prepare the French equivalent of a snack.

Elvis explained confidentially that in his time, Pierre had been one of the premier chefs in France. He had garnered a three-star rating but could never climb higher. That was the ultimate insult to a French chef, or saucier, as they were called. So he quit, and began a life of private employment.

Brigitte, Babette, Elvis and I salivated over a paté and legume concoction fashioned by Pierre. Believe me, no matter how unappetizing that sounds, it was delicious.

After finishing the meal, which we ate in the kitchen, Elvis asked me to join him in the foyer. While the girls gossiped in the garden, Pierre cleaned up the rustic kitchen.

Elvis seemed nervous. He hemmed and hawed, making small talk for about five minutes. Finally he asked me, "Doc, will you give me some advice?"

I stumbled a bit with my answer, although I felt extremely flattered. Suddenly, the girls ran past us, headed to the upstairs. It broke our concentration. Then he turned to me and asked,

"Have you ever been to the Eiffel Tower? I mean up on the observation deck?"

"No, I sure haven't. I'd like to." I said, a little puzzled.

"Come on then, you're in for a treat!"

Elvis explained to Pierre that he and I were going out for a bit.

"Tell the girls, will you?" he added.

We got in the Peugeot and headed out to the broad avenues of Paris. We could see the steel framework of the fabled landmark towering above this most romantic city of Gaul.

It's hard to imagine that when the Eiffel Tower was first completed, it was considered an eyesore. As we puttered along, I was tempted...no, I was dying to ask Elvis what was on his mind, but I didn't dare. I didn't want to spoil the mood.

When we arrived at the Tower, the usual crush of tourists were everywhere. No wonder the French and other Europeans laugh at Americans—we look like a bunch of clowns! There's no mistaking an American tourist, that's for sure.

We waited our turn and then rode up to the observation deck. When we got there, we took several minutes to simply look out at the beautiful city below us. It was almost dusk and lights were beginning to twinkle here and there.

"What do you think I should do about Babette?" Elvis asked after several minutes of silence.

The question took me a little by surprise. He was such a private person, and this was the kind of question you would ask your best friend, not someone that you had known a week or so. I think it indicated the depth of his isolation and loneliness.

"Elvis," I finally mumbled, "it depends. Do you love her? Do you want to build a life with her?"

He hesitated, then looked at me with sad eyes.

"Doc, I don't know."

He hesitated again. Then something seemed to snap and his countenance changed entirely.

"Sorry," he said. "I have to make a decision. You understand, don't you?"

I nodded my understanding. I decided it was

better to say nothing at that point.

"Hey," he began, looking around the near-empty observation deck.

"Why don't you pick up the story in Nashville. What did Red the lawyer advise you to do?"

So on the observation deck of Paris' most famous landmark, I began to recount the story of the weekend before the court hearing. I completed the story I had begun in the bar as fully and completely as I could.

* * * * *

"Son," Red began," I don't think you have any choice but to testify. But..."

"But what," I shot back.

"I would strongly recommend that you obtain legal counsel!"

"You mean you, don't you?"

"That's your choice, Dr. St. John. Let me point out if the state is persuaded by law or other cause to do this dastardly thing, you will probably not be held liable. After all, you'll be doing your job. But if I were in your shoes, I would want a lawyer to guide me through these difficult times."

I had to hand it to the old red fox. Even though he looked like a shyster and probably was one, there was never a smarter or smoother-tongued devil.

I hesitated as I tried to think clearly. The beer had dulled my senses.

"What's in this for you, Red?" I finally blurted out.

"Money, of course. I'll give you a listing of my charges. But that's not the main reason I want to represent you."

"What is the reason then?"

"Celebrity, notoriety, fame...whatever you want to call it. Do you have any idea how much publicity is going to be generated by this? I want to be in the middle of this thing."

"Hey, I told you this is all top-secret."

"It won't be for long. This will get out, I guarantee it. It'll be the event of the century if the state proceeds to disinter the remains of Elvis Presley..." He stopped and brushed the thinning shock of red hair above both ears.

"And you, Dr. St. John, will be at the center of this fire storm. To be honest, I've never even heard of something like this happening."

His astute point made me ponder the prospect of being on the stand without counsel. As soon as that thought crossed my mind, I decided to hire Red on the spot. After all, I didn't have much time to seek out other legal advice. This had hit me all of a sudden. I didn't know what else to do. Although Dr. Regent would be there, Marcia wouldn't. I needed support!

"What can you foresee happening if this comes to pass, I mean if I have to supervise the exhumation?"

"The Presley estate could hold you personally liable." He shrugged his shoulders as if to indicate that he would not guarantee me anything one way or the other.

"Okay...okay...be there Monday as my counsel; hopefully the state will come to their senses on this thing."

Red broke into a big smile. He shook my hand vigorously.

"I think we should spend the rest of the weekend getting to know each other and getting prepared for the trial."

"Why?" was all I could think of to ask.

"Because it's been my experience that the better prepared my client is, the better off he'll be in the courtroom. But it's late. Why don't we all get some rest and meet in the morning for breakfast. We can discuss everything then. Let's meet at ten a.m. at the restaurant in the Hermitage."

"Okay," I agreed. I didn't know what else to do. I shook Red's hand and said good night to Daisy.

Robert Mickey Maughon, M.D.

Chapter Nineteen

I was a lonely man as I walked from Second Avenue back to the hotel that night. I walked through the old refurbished lobby of the Hermitage hotel. It had been elegantly redone. The oldness of the place somehow made me feel less important.

I had a restless sleep that night. Visions of the courtroom, even of the graveside at Graceland haunted me. Although all of this was not my doing, I still felt responsible for some reason.

Ten o'clock finally came. Mercifully, I would now at least have a game plan for my presentation Monday. What that would be, I didn't know.

I met Red in the lobby restaurant. He was already eating a huge cheese and green pepper omelet with wheat toast.

"I was hungry," he said, his red hair glistening in the reflected sun in the room.

"I hope you don't mind that I went ahead and ate."

"No, not at all," I said. I ordered the same meal from the waitress. "Did Daisy not come?" I asked.

"Naw, she had to go to church. Never misses a Sunday, that one."

Red didn't miss a beat as he ate and

simultaneously spoke. "The way I see this, Doc, if you have to testify at the hearing, all you can do is give the knowledge that you have at hand."

The waitress brought my breakfast. I dug in as the beer from the night before had given me an appetite.

"I've never done a postmortem on a body that has been buried this long. To be quite honest, Red, I don't know what to tell them to expect. I'm not sure if anything can be learned or not. Sure, I can tell them what I've read in textbooks, but as far as my personal experience goes, it will be sheer speculation."

Red finished his food. He looked at me straight in the eye.

"I know all of that!" he said.

"Then why are you here?" I asked.

"I told you last night, the notoriety and all that. I know, I know...why do you as the medical examiner of Memphis need a lawyer there if that's all there is to it? I'll tell you why. Because there may be something screwy asked—something that catches you off guard and that you shouldn't answer!"

"Like what?" I asked.

"Doctor, this is the strangest thing I have ever heard of. And believe me I have been around some crazy stuff. If you were my relative, I would advise you to obtain top-grade legal counsel at this thing. Who knows what's going to happen? I'm just advising you to be cautious. Of course, if you want to go at this thing alone..." His voice trailed off.

"No, no...I would feel better with someone on my side. After all, I'm not real sure why they need me here at all. It seems to me that DELTA Records and the Presley estate will be going at it, not me."

"That may be so, and that sound reasonable, but what if you get all embroiled in a big mess?"

I knew Red was right. He had picked up on my insecurity of testifying in court. What did they want from me, anyway? Yes, I would definitely feel better if someone who had my best interest at heart was there in the courtroom.

"Okay," I said, "What do you need to know? Or rather what is it that we need to talk about?"

With that Red and I began to explore all the possibilities of the nature of the questioning. We had coffee and more coffee. Red touched on all sorts of points concerning the legalities of exhuming a body. For example, what if there were jewelry on the corpse. What kind of steps would the coroner's office take to ensure its safety? Red brought up all kinds of peculiar things that I wouldn't have thought of. Would hints of drugs or even poison still show up?

Red and I had the whole weekend to talk. By the time Monday morning came around, I felt prepared, or as prepared as one could be for something like this.

* * * * *

The observation deck was thinning out as I continued to tell my story to Elvis. Night was settling over Paris. The lights of the city began to come alive. The Eiffel Tower somehow began to resemble a giant carnival ride. All the city's traffic and the bustle below seemed to make it move.

Elvis looked at me. "I still don't understand. Why did they want to do this in the first place?"

"Well, the best way to explain is to tell you what happened at the hearing. Of course I cheated a bit by telling you what someone else had told me about Giorgio Enricci."

Elvis gave a noncommittal shrug.

"I can't remember what I ever did to that guy." But then a devilish smile took over his face.

"What is it ?"I asked.

He looked downward in a shy manner. "I think I know who that girl might be," he finally said.

"You're kidding!" I had gotten to know him well enough now to be fairly forthright. I looked at him expectantly, pleading with my eyes for him to tell me.

"Who?" I finally asked. "For heaven's sakes, tell me. She better be pretty special, because from everything I learned, she evidently was the main reason Georgi Enricci had held such a grudge against you."

Elvis' shy smile faded and his expression turned to one of concern. He didn't say anything.

"Who was it?"

"Ann-Margret."

My mouth flew open. But it made sense. Las Vegas. The sixties. I nodded my head up and down in understanding.

If it was indeed Ann-Margret, she would be woman enough to make a man hold a grudge against another man for a lifetime. Hell, for Ann-Margret, a lifetime might not be long enough.

"That would explain it, pal!" I didn't elaborate. After all he probably felt bad enough without my reminding him of the trouble he had brought, to a certain degree anyway, onto himself.

"Come on, let's go." He grabbed my arm and

walked me to the elevator and away from the observation deck.

We watched the traffic and lights sparkle around us on the way down. Darkness fell rapidly as we descended. I started to pick back up where I'd stopped in the story, but he said to wait till we got back to the townhouse. He evidently wanted to enjoy nighttime in Paris.

We decided to walk home. It was just too perfect of an evening not to. We could pick up the Peugeot in the morning. It was amazing how crowded the city had become. Two weeks earlier when I had met him at the little bar, Paris had seemed like a ghost town to me. I was probably so engrossed in finally seeing and meeting Elvis that it just seemed that way.

Tonight the streets were packed. We constantly bumped into couples, old men and an occasional woman of the evening. Even though our progress was slow, we enjoyed the walk immensely. Neither one of us said a lot, as we were enjoying the night so much. At one point we passed the shell of a shop that had been bombed by religious extremists. This was an event that had become way too common in the past few years in Paris.

"I don't understand those people," I reckoned as we passed the charred remnants.

"Dangerous nuts," was all Elvis said as we walked by.

We continued on in silence. When we arrived back at the townhouse, it was fairly late.

Pierre greeted us with an offer of a late-night snack. We both declined. The girls had already gone to bed. I wondered to what extent my relationship had evolved with Brigitte. Elvis and I said good night; he directed me to the guest bedroom, a small corner room beyond Pierre's.

As I entered the room, a sliver of moonlight coming through the window revealed the small, fragile outline of Brigitte curled up in bed. It seemed so comfortable sliding in and cuddling with her warm form. I felt at home.

The next morning greeted us when a slip of sunlight entered the room. Brigitte and I had said hello to each other by making love during the night. We jumped from bed, cleaned up, dressed and ran downstairs.

Pierre was busy in the kitchen getting breakfast. His constantly smiling old face would make anyone feel at home. Babette soon joined us at the table. She and Brigitte began to excitedly plan a day out shopping.

"Let's go to the Champs Elysses," Babette said to Brigitte in her thick French accent.

"Oui, mais certainement," Brigitte declared as she smiled at me.

I silently hoped Elvis and I would be able to stay behind. I finally had his full interest and attention in my story and felt he would be ready to continue this morning.

Finally Elvis appeared at the table. He was greeted by an affectionate Babette. Their earlier spat apparently had been totally forgotten.

When we were approached by the two girls, intent on shopping, we deftly explained we would wait here at the house in order to help Pierre. That elicited a small laugh from Brigitte and a louder laugh from Pierre. His response made us all laugh. It was apparent that the guys didn't want to go shopping.

It didn't take long for the girls to get ready and run out the door, exclaiming that we didn't know what we were missing.

Elvis and I laughed, and headed out to the garden. No longer did I feel obligated to ask his permission or wait for him to ask me to begin the story. I just began up where I left off.

* * * * *

Monday morning, Red accompanied me to the courthouse. The governor had finally contacted me and given me the details on where to go and when. We entered the large marble building and headed to the main chamber.

A uniformed officer asked me what my business was there. I told him about the hearing and explained that Red Shaugnessy was my lawyer. He looked at a short list of people on a clipboard. He grunted, "here you are," as he jabbed at my name with his stubby finger. The guard then led us through several rooms to a door, where he nodded to another guard who in turn led us into a small chamber that resembled a mini-courtroom.

The small room was packed with about twenty people. I had no idea where to sit. Was I a witness for the family or the record company. I guess in reality, I would be called as an expert witness. My role in this matter was definitely confusing. I wanted the Presley family to know that I was on their side. I spotted Priscilla up front, with what I assumed was a bevy of her lawyers.

I explained to Red that I wanted to go and talk with her. He interjected decidedly that now was not the time. I must admit, having Red with me made me feel much better.

* * * * *

"How did DELTA Records convince the judge to exhume my body or what was supposed to be my body?" a spellbound Elvis excitedly asked as Pierre interrupted us, asking us if we needed anything. We declined.

I smiled. Elvis had been so reticent at first to talk about this, and now I had his undivided attention...and his curiosity.

"Elvis, hold your horses. It's bizarre, but that old Cherokee law was key. You're getting way ahead of the story."

His enthusiasm embarrassed him momentarily. He caught himself, realizing that he was indeed becoming intrigued by this unusual story. He smiled softly.

"Sorry. Go on," he said with a sheepishly.

* * * * *

A bailiff entered the room and said, "All rise."

Everyone in the courtroom immediately hushed and stood at attention. A gray-haired, black-robed judge emerged from a side door and entered the courtroom. He walked to the bench and sat down.

Everyone sat down and a stirring of papers and whispering filled the air. At one table sat the attorneys for Winston Doyle and DELTA Records. At the other were Priscilla and the attorneys for the Presley estate. The attorneys at both tables were busy comparing notes and strategies.

Dr. Regent was seated in front of us. He finally turned and spotted me. Smiling, he got up and made his way back to me and Red.

Robert Mickey Maughon, M.D.

He explained that he had just driven in from Memphis. I introduced Red and Dr. Regent. Dr. Regent allowed that it wasn't a bad idea for me to have legal representation there, but he didn't really think it was necessary since I would be only an expert witness.

Finally an officer of the court stood up and stated in a loud voice, "The case of DELTA Records versus the Estate of Elvis Aron Presley will come to order."

The judge, who I later learned was Riley Comer, a retired judge who had served for more than forty years, slammed his gavel down and began, "Will the attorneys for both sides approach the bench?"

We were unable to hear what transpired between the judge and the attorneys. Judge Comer was slightly animated as his wrinkled, prune-like face drew into a frown of disapproval. He seemed to be admonishing both sides in a very stern manner. Finally the attorneys walked back to their respective tables.

Judge Comer then addressed the audience, "We will hear first from the attorney for DELTA Records."

As both sides prepared for their opening statements, the courtroom filled with a low buzz of anticipation. The noise grew to such a level that the judge slammed his gavel in protest. The noise subsided somewhat.

A lawyer arose from the table where Winston Doyle and his DELTA Record cronies sat. He strode to the front of the room and addressed the courtroom.

I found out later that the attorney who began to speak was from the Washington law firm of

Burgess and Harrison, a highly prestigious firm but one without principles. His name was Jerry Zimmer, and he was tall, thin, blonde and arrogant.

As he began, his chest swelled out and he paced in front of the judge's bench.

"Your honor," he stated, "we will show that the estate of Elvis Aron Presley has defrauded my client, DELTA Records, out of millions of dollars of royalties. We will prove that this has occurred due to the fact that in actuality, Elvis Aron Presley is not dead."

At that moment Priscilla Presley jumped up, sobbing. She was led from the courthouse by a gentleman in his seventies whom I didn't recognize.

* * * * *

I paused and looked over at Elvis. His face was cringed in anger, but he looked at me and said simply, "Go on."

* * * * *

Jerry Zimmer seemed to relish the effect he had on her. It made me hate him instantly. He reminded me of a little bantam rooster who thought he was whole lot more important than he was.

He continued: "What we will prove is that the Presley estate took millions of dollars from DELTA Records, even though they knew that it is possible that Elvis Aron Presley is not buried at Graceland, as they have stated."

"What we intend to prove is that Elvis Presley is not buried at Graceland as the estate has maintained. We will present five witnesses who will give sworn testimony that they have seen Elvis

Robert Mickey Maughon, M.D.

Presley since August 1977. We will then request the court to act under Tennessee Law #100745-A9 and to order the exhumation of the body at the site where the Presley estate has said the remains are buried."

Red looked at me and Dr. Regent. "Well, the shit has definitely hit the fan now!" he said in his classic, understated style.

Chapter Twenty

"Hi! We're back." Babette and Brigitte burst into the room. They brought instant enthusiasm wherever they went, and I was glad. Have you ever had to tell someone something bad, like about a death in the family? It makes you feel like a jerk. I had to do that on occasion as an ER doc. It's no fun. That why I was so glad that the girls were back. They would bring sunshine to any room.

When I was telling Elvis the courtroom story, his face was so sad. It twisted into anger when I told him about Priscilla. Now he was smiling again as Babette curled up on his lap.

I didn't want to make him sad, but I'm sure he would demand to hear the rest of the story. Strangely, I didn't want to tell him the rest of this crap.

Seeing Elvis and Babette so happy together made me feel bad. I had come into his life and brought a sad story. A tale of a life he had gone to extraordinary measure to escape. I felt like an intruder, and it was not a good feeling.

Brigitte was hugging me around my neck. She had noticed my sad countenance and was trying to cheer me up. She said something hurriedly in

French to Babette, who then whispered something into Elvis' ear.

When he looked at me, the sad face of fifteen minutes earlier was gone.

"Cheer up, Dr. St. John! I'm a big boy." I took his slow smile as a sign that he was not going to blame me for the message I was bringing. After all, I was just the messenger.

Pierre walked into the room and mumbled something in that low tone of his. Almost immediately, Babette and Brigitte shouted, *"Oui, oui!"*

I looked at Elvis quizzically.

"Pierre wants us to have a cook-out on the rooftop." Elvis went on to explain that the roof of the flat-topped, three-story town house made a great place to have a picnic in the summer.

"We'll use a hibachi as our camp fire," he said.

All of us swooped around in the house, helping Pierre take various ingredients to the top of the roof. A small glass-topped table was pushed off to the side, close to one ledge. The coals in the red-hot hibachi glowed. A couple of small fondue pots sat on top of the grill, and small tendrils of smoke waved above before slowly evaporating into the Paris night.

A better vantage point to gaze over our side of the city couldn't have been had. We took turns at each side of the building, viewing the distant sights and sounds of this city of lights before settling down to conversation.

Babette cuddled back into Elvis' arms, Brigitte into mine. Crowds of people could be heard two streets over as they walked about, enjoying the sights of Paris. The July night was bright not only

Elvis Is Alive

from the lights of the city but also from the stars, which hovered beautifully overhead. The whole atmosphere exuded romance.

Babette hurriedly spoke of her ideas for us over the next weekend or so. She wanted us to go back to the beach house. But first, why not a day trip to London through the new "Chunnel." She mentioned several other little expeditions that she wanted to take us on: the wine country, the palace at Versailles, and Notre Dame.

"We will have so much fun!" she explained to all of us.

It was easy to get caught up in her enthusiasm. Brigitte punched me playfully on the arm every other word, trying to nudge me into saying yes to all of the fun activities her cousin was conjuring up for us to enjoy.

Pierre began to bring us small samplings from his fondue pots: wrapped lamb in bacon strips and mushrooms, deep-fried in olive oil. Everything Pierre cooked was wonderful.

Before long, we were all satiated. Pierre had slowly treated us to supper without our really paying attention. He brought tidbit after tidbit until after forty-five minutes or so we had been fed a complete meal. Never were we disrupted from our conversation or ideas of having fun. I guess that was the French host in him. Pierre's skill made a simple night on a rooftop in Paris seem extraordinarily special.

Our laughter carried across town, I am sure. As Pierre poured us glasses of Chardonnay, we slid back into a more relaxed series of conversations. Babette leaned up against Elvis. Brigitte snuggled against me. The embers from the grill emitted various shades of red lights, which brightened our smiling, laughing faces.

Brigitte and Babette turned from planning our next few days to telling funny anecdotes about their family. A cousin did this, an uncle who lived near Nice did that. They kept us entertained with their quaintly humorous stories. From what they were saying, I didn't see much difference in the way their family behaved from the way I perceived mine did. Eventually, Babette and Brigitte huddled together to trade their own stories and plans; these two were very close. I now considered it a conspiracy of sorts that I had been paired with Brigitte.

True, we were a very good match, compatible in most every way. But when I saw the two of them giggling and laughing together, I realized that it was indeed a planned event that I had been introduced to Brigitte. Of course, who could have resented being matched to such a beautiful young lady? Especially when I saw how she and Babette truly enjoyed being together. I realized how much their laughter and caring for each other was contagious. It made wherever they were a fun place to be.

Pierre brought Elvis and me a strong, heated cognac. We wandered away from the girls, leaving them to their own company, and we walked over to the ledge that overlooked the garden. It gave us some privacy and a chance to continue our talk. In a way I dreaded continuing, but there was no turning back now.

"Tell me about the rest of the court proceedings." Elvis took a sip of his after dinner cordial, never looking me in the eye. He simply stared into the courtyard.

"Are you sure?" I felt telling the rest of the story was inevitable, and I felt the tale had now reached critical mass. I knew he wanted to hear the rest; it was too late to turn back.

I took a slow sip of cognac. Its rich flavor was addictive.

"Hmm," I sighed, partly from the flavor of the drink and partly from trying to remember the next scene of the Nashville courtroom.

"Jerry Zimmer. Jerry Zimmer," I remembered as I took another sip. "He presided over the whole affair."

* * * * *

Jerry was wandering around the front of the courtroom with a big smile on his face, just like the cat who ate the yellow canary. All the emotion in the world was breaking loose in that courtroom and he seemed to love it! He put his hands in his colorful suspenders that were covered with Snoopy, Charlie Brown, the Red Baron and Woodstock. He then continued his opening statement under the watchful eye of Judge Riley Comer.

"Your Honor and ladies and gentlemen. I, as a representative of DELTA Records, intend to prove to the court that Elvis Aron Presley is not dead. We will achieve this by the statements of five credible eyewitnesses to the fact that is impossible for Elvis to be buried at Graceland, as Elvis is alive."

This outlandish statement and his behavior elicited a rustle of noise from the limited number of witnesses in the courtroom. Judge Comer tapped his gavel again to quieten the noise.

* * * * *

After he finished his opening statement, the

judge called for a fifteen-minute break. No one left the small courtroom, though; people continued to talk among themselves.

After the break, Judge Comer told Jerry Zimmer to call his first witness. He walked back and forth in front of the judge's bench for at least a minute, then finally took a deep breath, and turning to the courtroom audience, said, "DELTA Records calls Beverly Kaye Simms as its first witness."

The bailiff stood up and called, "Beverly Kaye Simms, please approach the bench to be seated and sworn in."

A short, bleached-blonde woman in a tight fighting black suit rose from the back pew and clunked down the aisle to the witness stand.

She was probably fifty-plus years old and wore a lot of dark make-up and hair spray. The bailiff asked her name. She placed her hand with long purple-painted fingernails on the Bible.

"I am Beverly Kaye Simms, your honor," the plump, beach blonde proudly and boldly declared.

She must have had trouble following his instructions as she shouted, "I do," as the bailiff finished with "...so help you God."

Zimmer hovered around the witness, alternately looking at the members of the audience and the judge, "Ms. Simms, will you tell us how and when you knew Elvis Aron Presley?"

She squirmed in the chair a bit and puffed her hair with those awful fingernails. Her bleached hair and her purple fingernails provided an incredible contrast. Finally she stopped primping long enough to look over at Judge Comer, batted her eyes, and in one of the strongest Southern accents you can imagine said, "I was his lover from 1980 until 1984."

Muffled cries of disbelief and astonishment shivered throughout the court room. Judge Comer smashed his gavel down, "Order in this court!" he demanded.

The witness nonchalantly observed her fingernails and picked a long strand of bleached blonde hair off her bosom, flicking it to the floor.

"Are you sure?" Zimmer finally asked, as the noise in the courtroom subsided. Everyone, including Judge Comer, seemed to lean forward to get a better view of this woman and to hear her answer.

"Sure, I'm sure," she replied, looking at Jerry Zimmer as if he were crazy.

"How do you know it was Elvis Presley?"

Again looking at him with disdain, she said, "It was Elvis Presley. We lived together in Las Vegas for that period of time."

* * * * *

I paused for a moment to look at Elvis out of the corner of my eye. He was sitting on the corner of the ledge staring back over at the girls. I looked back over my shoulder at them. They were busy with their own conversation and were not paying any attention to us.

"Did you know her, this witness Beverly Kaye Simms?" I whispered at Elvis, even though I knew the girls couldn't hear me.

"Are you nuts! Never heard of her!" His face contorted in contempt.

"Sorry," I sighed under my breath. "She was a

pretty convincing witness, no matter how she looked."

"Go on," Elvis urged, obviously engrossed in her testimony.

I laughed inadvertently, as I recalled Beverly Kaye Simms' bleached blonde image in my mind's eye.

* * * * *

Jerry Zimmer took a couple of minutes to walk around the front of the courtroom. It seemed as if he wanted to extract every ounce of the spotlight that he could. He pulled and tugged on his suspenders so much that Snoopy and his gang seemed to tap dance on top of his chest.

"How can you be sure it was the real Elvis Presley?" he asked, his words softly building to a crescendo. He turned and faced the audience for effect as he awaited her answer.

Beverly Kaye Simms puffed her hair with her long fingernails again. She too seemed to pause before answering.

"Honey, when a woman sleeps with a man for nearly five years, she sure as hell knows who he is! Do you think I would stay with a man that long if he just PRETENDED to be Elvis?"

Jerry Zimmer then turned to the judge.

"Your Honor, this is the first witness who will testify that she actually knew Elvis Aron Presley after the time that the attorneys for the Elvis Presley estate say he died."

With that, attorney Zimmer sat back down next to his client, Winston Doyle. Winston looked around the room and smiled at the crowd.

The attorney for the Presley estate, Carl Evans,

stood up. He wore a conservative blue suit. For some reason, he did not attack the credibility of the witness as I thought he should. He approached her and in a low-key voice asked only a couple of simple questions: Where did she live and how did she meet Elvis? That sort of thing. It was so subtle that I have a hard time remembering what he said. Suddenly he stopped and told Judge Comer that he was through questioning the witness.

A buzz now circled the small courtroom. What was the Presley estate's strategy? Why weren't they more aggressive? Surely, they had a plan. After all, the veracity of this witness could easily be called into question.

Judge Comer addressed the witness, "You may step down."

Beverly Kaye Simms exited from the witness stand as if she had given the testimony of a lifetime, which for her, she probably had.

Jerry Zimmer bounced up from the seat beside Winston Doyle.

"Your Honor, our next witness to testify is Mary Ann Simms."

An older woman from the back suddenly stood up and began her trek forward to the witness seat. She looked like an older version of Beverly Kaye Simms, except that she had to use a cane to support herself. She walked with a slight limp.

When she had reached the witness stand, she placed her cane next to the railing so everyone could see it.

'When did you know Elvis Presley?" Jerry Zimmer started.

"The same time as my daughter."

"So, you knew that the man who was involved

with your daughter, Beverly Kaye, was Elvis Aron Presley?"

"Oh, yes sir. We knew. He didn't want us to tell anyone that he was Elvis, but he was. There is no doubt in my mind! My daughter and I confide in each other about everything."

Jerry Zimmer didn't push the questioning any harder. He asked her how her daughter had met this man, how long they had known each other, that sort of thing.

After the questioning he turned to Carl Evans and said, "Your witness."

Again inexplicably, Carl Evans carried on a very low-key interrogation of the witness. No hard rebuttal. No slashing questions of, "What do you hope to gain from all of this?"

After a few routine questions, he dismissed the witness from the stand.

It was now noon, and the judge instructed the two benches and the rest of the courtroom that there would be a one-hour recess before court reconvened at one p.m. Before Judge Comer dismissed us he stood and shook his gavel at each and everyone.

"I want to admonish everyone who is present that there will be absolutely no discussion with any party that is not privy to these proceedings. This is considered to be a "gag order." I will not allow anyone to violate this. You do not even want to know the severity of my punishment if my instructions are not followed to the letter. Does everyone understand?"

The participants simply nodded their heads.

Judge Comer yelled loudly, "Does everyone understand!"

A collective, "Yes, sir," arose from the courtroom. Then everyone rushed hurriedly from the room. Dr. Regent, Red and I hustled down the street to Tootsie's Orchid Lounge. None of us were hungry. We just wanted a place to sit and have a drink. A place to discuss the curious nature of Carl Evans' defense.

Red said he was flabbergasted.

"This doesn't make sense!" he said. "According to that screwy law, if Zimmer can get three more eyewitnesses to testify in court that Elvis is indeed alive, Judge Comer has no choice but to have the body exhumed."

"Maybe that's it." He scratched his head as he talked to no one in particular.

"What do you mean?" I asked.

"Well, I think that maybe the Presley estate has accepted the inevitable and realizes that DELTA can probably get thousands of kooky types of people to testify that they've seen Elvis. Maybe they're resigned to having the body exhumed and getting this whole thing over with!"

"That makes me sad," Dr. Regent countered as he took a swig of his Bud Light.

"I agree." Red shook his head.

"But what does DELTA hope to get if they have the body exhumed?" I asked in exasperation.

Red Shaugnessy looked at me. Half in jest and half in seriousness he wiggled those infernal red eyebrows up and down and in an exaggerated manner. "Maybe they know something we don't!"

Robert Mickey Maughon, M.D.

Chapter Twenty-One

When we had settled into our seats after the recess, Judge Comer reentered the courtroom to, "All rise."

He looked at Jerry Zimmer and simply nodded, implying that it was time for the next witness.

Jerry jumped up and turned around. He said with a flourish, "We call as our next witness, Jeb V. Stencil."

A sixtyish-looking man dressed in overalls and a stiffly starched white shirt approached the witness stand.

After he took his seat, the bailiff swore him in with his hand placed on the Bible. This was difficult due to the fact that the man's hand shook from some type of palsy.

"Mr. Stencil, you have sworn under oath in a deposition that you knew Elvis Aron Presley in 1989. Is this correct?

In a halting voice but one that exuded confidence, Jeb Stencil stated, "Yes sir, that's correct."

"How did you meet him?"

"I have a farm in Arkansas. There's an old road behind the back of my house down next to the barn. Well, one Saturday I was driving my ole '39

Elvis Is Alive

Ford pick-up back down that road. Before I knew it a big green Cadillac rounded the corner and broadsided me. The man driving that Cadillac was Elvis Presley."

Jeb Stencil looked around the courtroom, daring anyone to question his statement.

Jerry Zimmer again tucked his hands under his suspenders, bouncing them up and down feverishly.

"Are you certain it was *the* Elvis Presley?" He looked back over his shoulder at the audience to magnify the importance of his question.

"Oh, yes sir. It was Elvis, all right. He got out of that big green Cadillac and said, 'I'm Elvis Presley, don't you dare call your insurance company, they all think I'm dead.'"

That statement from Jeb brought a laugh form the courtroom; even Judge Comer smiled although he tried to hide it with his gavel as he called for order. Jeb then continued his story.

"Then Elvis pulled out the most god-awful roll of hundred dollar bills from the pocket of the red velvet jump suit he was wearing and asked me, 'How much would it take to fix my vehicle?' He was about the nicest guy you would ever want to meet. I had recognized him instantly, of course." Jeb again looked menacingly around the room, daring anyone to laugh again or doubt his word.

"Of course, he asked that I not tell anybody, and I never did, nobody but my family and a few folks I could trust in town. That is, until I got this 'subpenie'." The old farmer crossed his arms over his barrel chest in defiance.

* * * * *

A cool breeze now wafted over the Paris rooftops. I looked over at Elvis. His arms were crossed over his chest also. He was now leaning back, his eyes closed. The hibachi, although nearly burned out, still cast a reddish glow against his face.

I couldn't help but ask, "Elvis, ever heard of this old bird?"

Elvis never opened his eyes. Without changing positions he simply said, "Are you kidding, I never liked red velvet." He laughed.

"Go on."

I shrugged and said, "Okay." I returned to my story.

* * * * *

Jerry Zimmer threw out his arms exultantly and turned to Carl Evans and said, "Your witness."

Attorney Evans walked to the witness stand.

"Are you sure, Mr. Stencil, that this was *the* Elvis Presley? There are a lot of impersonators out there, you know."

"Yes sir. I have no doubt. I've followed Elvis ever since he was a kid in Memphis. Besides, why would an impersonator pay me in cash and tell me not to tell anyone? Why wouldn't he just give me his insurance card? It took three-thousand dollars to fix my Ford. Elvis paid me in good cash money."

"No more questions, your honor," Carl Evans said over his shoulder as he resumed his seat at the estate's table.

The old farmer walked down the aisle back to his seat. He was grim-faced, having done his duty.

Jerry Zimmer smiled widely as he got up and approached the judge.

Elvis Is Alive

"Your honor, I will call as my next witness, Mr. Roy Roux.

A medium-built man with a large handlebar moustache arose from the middle of the courtroom. He slowly walked to the witness stand; his alligator boots made a tremendous clacking noise against the hardwood floor. The baliff approached to swear in the witness. Roy Roux assured everyone that he would tell the whole truth

Jerry Zimmer asked nonchalantly, "Mr. Roux, please tell the court where you were the night of June 16, 1993."

'Cajun Roy' began to roll the tips of his huge moustache with his fingers and looked up at the ceiling of the courtroom.

"Hmm," he pondered. Then in a very heavy Cajun accent he said, "I was in the company of the bodacious Ms. Shelia DuHon of Baton Rouge."

"NO! NO! Mr. Roux," Jerry Zimmer protested in a perturbed manner, "I meant around midnight that night, the reason you have been asked to testify here today."

"Oh, yes sir, you mean much later that night, out on the bayou."

Jerry Zimmer nodded his head in approval, "Yes, that's right, Mr. Roux, tell the court what happened much later that night out on the Louisiana Bayou."

"I was out in my hollowed-out cypress wood skiff hunting 'gators. It was pitch dark."

Cajun Roy took time to bring his eyes from the ceiling and surveyed the spectators, making sure he had our attention. This colorful man certainly had mine!

"Suddenly, the largest 'gator I have ever seen

attacked the skiff." Cajun Roy exclaimed as he made a large clapping noise with his outstretched hands, supposedly resembling an alligator's dangerous snout.

All of the audience jumped slightly at this explosion of sound. Cajun Roy smiled at the effect his story had had on his audience, then he continued in his strong drawl.

"I thought I was a goner." Cajun Roy shook his head, remembering that night. Unexpectedly, he jumped up from his chair and shouted, "Then Elvis appeared. He grabbed that ol' gator by the snout and twisted it so fast that it snapped its neck in two."

Cajun Roy sat back down and sighed deeply, "Any mortal man would have been taken down in that gator's death roll to the bottom of the swamp, but not Elvis Presley. He saved my life!"

Red turned to me and whispered, "What a crock of manure." I had to laugh.

Jerry Zimmer nodded triumphantly as if this testimony was the most valid he had ever heard. He sat down with Winston Doyle. A large contented smile seemed to cover his entire face.

Carl Evans did not rise from his chair. He simply waved his hand in a motion of sheer disbelief at Cajun Roy.

"No questions!"

Roy Roux stepped from the stand and loudly walked back to his place in the courtroom. He sat down. After adjusting his thick alligator boots, he began twirling both ends of his handlebar moustache.

Jerry Zimmer sprang back up from his seat. "Now, your honor, I will call our final witness."

Elvis Is Alive

Jerry stopped and looked around the courtroom as if he were searching for someone. His eyes lit up when he focused on a lady in her mid-forties. She had short brown hair. She was attractive, but not beautiful. Her dress and posture seemed to reveal that she was a professional or an executive.

This lady was in sharp contrast to the previous witnesses.

"I call to the stand, Ms. Rachel Alexander." Jerry Zimmer smiled his biggest smile of the hearing as the poised Ms. Alexander approached the stand.

The baliff swore in Mr. Zimmer's star witness as the courtoom fell silent.

Red leaned over to me and Dr. Regent and whispered, "Now this is starting to get a little weird. What in the world is someone like that doing here."

Red and I looked at Dr. Regent.

"What an attractive young woman," he said as he stared at the witness.

"Ms. Alexander, please tell the court something about yourself." Jerry Zimmer said, obviously in an attempt to accentuate her air of respectability.

Ms. Alexander cleared her throat and began talking in a clear, succinct manner.

"I work in the trust department of a large bank in Chicago. I was graduated Magna Cum Laude from Princeton University with a masters degree in Business Administration." Her personna exuded total credibility.

Red looked at Dr. Regent and me.

"Ohhhhhhh. Do you think she would have anything to do with me. The YMCA is my alma mater." Dr. Regent reluctantly took his eyes away from her momentarily and said, "Is that right."

Red and I couldn't help but laugh at his preoccupation with Ms. Rachel Alexander.

Jerry Zimmer approached the witness and said, "Ms. Alexander, will you please tell the court about your relationship with Elvis Aron Presley."

The spectators leaned forward to be able to hear every word this woman had to say.

"I was working at the bank one day in February of 1980. A handsome man came into the bank. He said he had a great deal of money to invest and he wanted my help. You can imagine how shocked I was when he said he was THE Elvis Presley."

Rachel paused a bit as her statement caused a stir of excitement from the audience.

"Order," Judge Comer said. He looked at the witness and smiled slightly.

"Go ahead with your testimony."

"Well, I am an educated woman. You can imagine my surprise at his statement. Then he produced absolute proof and documentation that he was Elvis Aron Presley." Rachel Alexander paused again before she continued.

"Go ahead, Ms. Alexander, tell us what your last name was for ten years." Jerry Zimmer demanded, his thumbs flipping those god-awful suspenders over and over.

"Well, from 1980 until 1990 my last name was not Alexander. I have retaken my maiden name after my divorce. You see, I was Elvis Presley's wife during that time."

A roar of disbelief arose from the audience. Judge Comer banged his gavel over and over and demanded order.

Beverly Kaye Simms arose from her seat in

the back of the courtroom and shouted, "You slutty liar!"

Her mother, Mary Ann Simms, stood up. She looked around for a soft place to fall, then she fainted.

"Come up here and call me that," the previously composed Rachel Alexander shouted at Beverly Kaye Simms.

Beverly Kaye pushed through the crowd and walked briskly to the front of the courtroom. She pointed a purple-colored index fingernail at the witness on the stand.

"How dare you say you were married to my man, Elvis. He loved me. He was gone a lot, to perform. He wasn't married to a slut like you though."

Dr. Regent, Red and I sat and watched this spectacle with open-mouthed astonishment.

The baliff and Jerry Zimmer tried to get between the two women. Both men were pushed aside as Beverly Kaye grabbed for Rachel Alexander and pulled her to the floor.

All sorts of obscenities were shouted as Beverly Kaye Simms and Rachel "Presley" Alexander fought on the floor of the Nashville courthouse. Each proclaimed Elvis' love as they took turns pulling each other's hair. It took several spectators to eventually separate the two brawling women.

It was a disgusted Judge Riley Comer who ordered the baliff to clear the two combatants from the courthouse.

None of this seemed to fluster Jerry Zimmer. He seemingly took in stride the fact that two of his eyewitnesses had beat the living daylights out of each other as they also directly contradicted each other's testimony about Elvis Presley. The more commotion that this farce of a hearing brought about seemed to delight him that much more.

"Well then, your honor," he began, "We would like to request…"

"Your honor," Carl Evans interrupted, "just because the Presley estate has not put up a spirited rebuttal of these…" he halted in mid-sentence, waving his arm over the crowd. "These so-called eyewitnesses does not mean that we rest. We would like to call a witness who cannot be here until tomorrow morning."

"Your honor?" Jerry Zimmer protested, obviously disappointed that he was not going to be able to close this out in one day.

Judge Riley Comer slammed his gavel down, interrupting Zimmer.

"We will recess until nine a.m.," he said.

The crowd erupted from their seats and headed to the back doors. Red, Dr. Regent and I decided to spend the afternoon together and have dinner. The conversation was an endless rendition of "Can you believe this? Disgusting! Why doesn't the estate put up a bigger fight? What a joke!" and "I wonder who the witness will be?"

We all agreed that the scenario was definitely like something out of a trashy novel. Dr. Regent repeatedly asked how I was doing and if I was holding up okay. He finally asked me what was really on his mind: Was I nervous about testifying?

Red ventured his opinion that the way the hearing was going I would not be asked to testify. I tended to agree. Red was of the opinion that the estate was not going to use a regular defense. He doubted I was going to have to give my so-called expert opinion. I agreed. After all, if the estate or DELTA Records had wanted me to testify, they would have called me by now.

It grew late, and I wanted to wander back to the Hermitage Hotel and go to sleep. I left Dr. Regent and Red Shaugnessy deep in argument over who the witness would be in the morning.

I settled into my room and called the front desk to ask for a wake-up call. I had a restless night filled with recurring dreams of my own death and funeral. I awoke on several occasions in a cold sweat. I was relieved when the hotel operator called me with my wake-up notice.

The next day was bright and sunny. Dr. Regent and Red were already seated when I entered the tiny courtroom. When I sat down by them, they continued their conversation, acknowledging me with only a quick glance with their eyes. Obviously they had become friends during the time they had spent with each other.

I noticed Jerry Zimmer pacing at the front of the room. He looked worried. I asked the guys what was up. A commotion at the side and back of the room answered my question. Priscilla Presley was ushered in by a host of people, including her attorney Carl Evans.

"What's up?" I repeated.

Red's eyebrows danced their mischievous dance. "The rumor is that Carl Evans and the estate team realizes that the law is on the side of DELTA Records. They're going to have Priscilla give an emotional appeal to Judge Comer."

"That's why Carl Evans didn't fight much yesterday."

Red paused and gave a low, almost inaudible,

"whoa." He looked at me and then at Dr. Regent.

"Boys, it's going to be a wild one today."

The bailiff entered the room and bellowed, "All rise."

Judge Riley Comer briskly strode to his desk. He allowed everyone to be seated, then shuffled a stack of papers in front of him. Red whispered that he was stalling for some reason. The courtroom became exceptionally quiet. Finally, Judge Comer looked directly at attorney Carl Evans.

"I understand you have a witness to call before I make my decision in this matter."

Carl Evans slowly rose and looked down at the group of people at his table, including Priscilla. He walked to the area in front of the judge's bench, where he turned and looked directly at Winston Doyle and Jerry Zimmer. He then turned to the audience, which seemed to be holding its collective breath, awaiting his speech.

The shy, somewhat discouraged person who was present yesterday was now gone. In his place was an energized, vibrant Carl Evans. His face turned bold and resolute.

"Yesterday," Carl Evans began slowly, "we listened to several people who spoke what they felt was the truth, but the truth at times is elusive. Today, someone will rebut that testimony. But before I call that witness…" Carl's face turned serious as he continued. He stepped up and looked directly at Jerry Zimmer.

"I want to say that today I am ashamed of the legal profession, a profession I am also deeply in love with." He stopped in mid-sentence.

He continued to stare at Jerry Zimmer when he said, "Your honor, I call as a witness, Priscilla Presley."

Priscilla Presley stood up and briskly walked to the witness stand.

Carl Evans waited to speak until after the bailiff had sworn in the witness. He then began, "Mrs. Presley, on behalf of all Tennesseans, I first want to say how ashamed I am that you and your family are having to go through this."

Priscilla Presley smiled slightly.

"Mrs. Presley, I want to ask you one question and one question only. Is there any doubt in your mind that your former husband, Elvis Presley, is deceased?"

Priscilla Presley had the audience spellbound. She looked around the room. It seemed as if a decade passed. Her head held high, she looked directly at Jerry Zimmer. Finally she spoke, clearly and without hesitation, "No sir, there is no question in my mind that my former husband, Elvis Aron Presley, is indeed deceased."

You could hear a pin drop. Carl Evans didn't say anything else. He took his seat.

Priscilla got up and began to walk back to her seat. Jerry Zimmer hopped up and excitedly said, "Wait, Mrs. Presley. I have some questions."

Priscilla Presley didn't break stride. She pointed an extended index finger at him and snarled, "Shut up and sit down!"

A giggle waved through the crowd as Jerry Zimmer slunk back down in his seat like a "whipped pup."

"Okay," he mumbled.

Carl Evans hugged Priscilla and turned back to the judge.

"Your honor, we have nothing else."

Judge Comer took a huge sigh. He rumbled

through the stack of papers, loudly shuffling them. He looked at Winston Doyle and Jerry Zimmer. A look of disgust came over his face. He continued to huff and sigh. He looked at Carl Evans and Priscilla Presley. He smiled a weak compassionate smile.

He looked directly down at the audience as he began to speak slowly and deliberately.

"Before I reveal my decision, I am issuing a gag order in this case. I will not tolerate the nature of these proceedings to be displayed over the front pages of the nation's newspapers. If anyone violates my order, they will be cited for contempt and will be incarcerated for no less than a year and fined no less than one million dollars."

The judge looked solemnly around the room.

"Does everyone here understand?"

A low mumuring of "yes sir" arose from the audience.

"Does everyone here UNDERSTAND!" The tone of his voice made the hairs on the back of my neck stand up as I knew he meant exactly what he said.

"YES SIR!" Everyone shouted in unison.

"Okay then," he declared when he was satisfied that his gag order was going to be obeyed. Judge Comer paused and then he cleared his throat.

"Today I am going to have to do something that frankly, I detest."

I imagined I saw tears well up in his eyes. I know for sure they became red-rimmed. He looked back down at his desk. The courtroom was deathly quiet.

"But...." He paused for a long time.

"Tennessee Law #100745-A9 states that in a case such as this, a case where there is a dispute

Elvis Is Alive

of monetary property and the deceased has been said to be alive in open court, contrary to all common sense," the old judge wavered, his voice breaking, "I have no choice in this matter but to find, no matter how reluctantly, in favor of Mr. Winston Doyle and DELTA Records and to order that the body of Elvis Aron Presley be exhumed for autopsy."

There was no protest from the Presley estate's bench. The other bench didn't celebrate, although Jerry Zimmer did turn and smile at everyone. His smile disappeared when a wadded-up piece of paper was thrown from the audience and hit him squarely on the end of his nose. That illicited an appreciative laugh from everyone.

The laughter subsided rapidly though, and the crowd filed out of the courtroom in an orderly fashion, much as if they had been at a funeral.

Chapter Twenty-Two

I looked back at Elvis. The red glow was gone from his face as the coals in the fire had finally died down. The girls had fallen into an unusual silence. They were looking over the top of the roof at the lights of Paris. We could still hear the sound of voices from the street, although they had mostly quieted down now.

Pierre had cleared the table and had gone downstairs. We agreed to go and sit downstairs with him. When we got there, Babette and Brigitte gravitated to the kitchen. Elvis and I went to the courtyard and sat down. Within minutes Pierre brought us some coffee. Elvis looked at me as he drank.

"Tell me what happened in Memphis," he said.

That was it. He was not very emotional about the whole thing. That had amazed me the whole time, his lack of emotion. I imagined it was a survival mechanism, considering he had to cope with leaving the life he had once lived. I continued the story with my trip back to West Tennessee.

* * * * *

Red decided to ride back to Memphis with Dr. Regent and me. It was a very crowded Jaguar XKE

Elvis Is Alive

that left Nashville. The trip down I-40 was a somber one. We discussed why the estate hadn't called the coroner who had performed the first autopsy. We went over a thousand things that we would have done differently.

Red kept saying, "There's more to this than we know."

When we arrived at Memphis, I went directly to my apartment. I had missed Marcia. When I to there, a surprise awaited me. Marcia welcomed me and then produced a registered letter. Winston Doyle and Jerry Zimmer had wasted no time after the hearing. They had an order signed by Judge Comer, which required that I, as the medical examiner of Shelby County, exhume the body of Elvis Presley, interred at Graceland, within the next seventy-two hours. I was to perform a postmortem and report the results immediately to Judge Comer, preferably within the week. These guys wasted no time. What jerks. I wanted to spend time with Marcia, but this news had taken me out of my amorous mood.

I rushed over to Dr. Regent's office with the registered letter containing the order. Red was still there. He looked at me with his large brown eyes, opened as wide as they could be.

"Wait 'till this gets around to Elvis' fans," he said.

"You're going to need police protection. There's no telling how much emotion is involved when it comes to Elvis. His fans could riot, you never know."

His bushy red eyebrows crawled up his worried, furrowed brow. His point was well taken.

The fans of Elvis Presley were known around

the world for their undying loyalty. Although the exhumation was supposed to be kept secret like the trial, word could slip out. Just wait until the fans heard what the judge had ordered. Just wait till they heard about the travesty perpetrated by those scum balls, Jerry Zimmer and Winston Doyle. Even though I was just going to do my job, I agreed with Red. This could be extremely dangerous. The more I thought about it, the more it scared me.

I immediately asked Dr. Regent to call the police chief, Willie Watson, to help me out.

Willie Watson was a native of Memphis and had played basketball for the Memphis Tigers. He was the first black police chief of Memphis and was very popular throughout the city. He was known for his colorful personality and his honesty.

Chief Watson told Dr. Regent to bring me down to the station to discuss the situation. Red accompanied us. When we arrived downtown at the police station, I didn't know what to expect.

Watson had played pro basketball for the Bullets for a season until he had torn up a knee. He was 6'9" and although he had been thin during his playing days, he had gained quite a bit of weight over the years. He wasn't fat, but he was a big man: formidable is probably a better word.

Red and Dr. Regent explained the situation we were in.

"I'll be damned," he said. "If anyone finds out about this, there's going to be a riot at Graceland!" He shook his head, not knowing what else to say.

Before we left the police station, the decision had been made to exhume the body that night. It was unanimous that the quicker we could get this over with, the better chance we would have of keeping it quiet.

* * * * *

I looked over at Elvis. As he had done the last couple of times I had continued with the story, he had closed eyes. Maybe he could concentrate better that way. Maybe the story was so emotional to him that he didn't want me to see his eyes. For whatever reason, he had his eyes closed with his back propped against the brick wall. He didn't look at me, but again said, "Go on."

* * * * *

When we left Chief Watson's office, the plan was to assemble at the South police station next to Graceland at nine p.m. Chief Watson would provide a police escort, and I was going to have a small crew to handle the earth removal. We would bring the casket back to the medical examiner's office and return it as soon as the postmortem was completed.

When we got there that night, the Chief Watson had ten officers gathered around him. He explained to them that no matter how despicable the action was, they had to keep personal feelings out of it and remember that they were only upholding the law.

We all got into police cars and a county hearse and headed up Elvis Presley Boulevard to Graceland. A guard stopped us at the gate, but opened it after Chief Wilson produced the court order. The chief instructed the guard to lock the gate behind us, then ordered his officers to guard the fence.

I thought the family might be there for one last attempt at stopping this insanity but Graceland actually looked deserted. The mayor, Chief Watson, Red, Dr. Regent and I walked back to the meditation garden where Elvis Aron Presley lay.

A sick feeling surged through my stomach as I ordered the workers to begin the work that would bring his casket to the light of day for the first time in twenty years.

I constantly checked over my shoulder to make sure no one was watching what we were doing through the fence, even though the police were doing a good job of guarding it.

It seemed to take forever to uncover the casket. No one in our group said anything. The workers finally finished their digging and brought the casket to the surface. They struggled through the red clay to take it to the hearse. Suddenly one of the workers stopped and ordered the others to lower the casket to the ground right in front of the opened back doors of the hearse.

He ran over to me. He was so agitated that I could barely understand what he was saying.

"Slow down," I told him. "I can't understand you!"

He kept saying, "Open it, open it," in a type of controlled, whispered scream.

I looked at his face and troubled eyes. There was something in his face that made me trust him. Since I was in charge I looked at the other workers and ordered, "Open it!"

Red Shaugnessy looked at me like I was crazy. He protested, "Not here, not now."

I looked back at the worker. For some crazy

reason, I trusted him.

He mouthed, "Open it," and nodded his head up and down to reassure me that it would be okay.

I walked forward and pulled the lid of the casket open.

Everyone gasped. The casket was empty.

Red Shaugnessy exclaimed, "Lord help us.........the king is risen."

Robert Mickey Maughon, M.D.

Chapter Twenty-Three

For some reason when I recalled the events of a year ago and recounted them to Elvis, I too would close my eyes. It helped me remember all the details. It always took me a couple of seconds to refocus my vision. When I returned my gaze to him, he was still leaning against the brick wall of the garden with his eyes closed also.

He got up and, looking at my cup, asked, "More coffee?"

"Sure," I muttered as he walked by and took my cup.

"I guess I have a lot of explaining to do," he said blandly as he walked back to the main part of the house.

For the first time since I had gotten to know him, I was irritated. If he had not wanted to go through this whole story, I had given him plenty of outs over the past couple of weeks.

I had just told him about digging up his vacant grave and he asked me if I wanted more coffee and said he reckoned I needed an explanation.

Hell yes, I think I finally deserved one. But it wasn't really that. It was his nonchalant attitude that bothered me. He must have noticed my agitation when he came back with my java.

"Don't mistake my coolness for indifference. If I allow myself to get too wrapped up in your story, I'll cry."

He motioned back toward the house.

"I don't want to upset the girls or Pierre."

I immediately felt like a jerk.

"Well, that pretty much ends the bulk of my story except for a few odds and ends," I said.

His eyes got wide.

"You haven't even told me about your following me for the last year."

"What about that?"

"I can tell you about that in, oh, fifteen minutes." I smiled. "It was simple in a way, but let me finally ask you something."

"Why?" I looked at Elvis with pleading, but with sympathetic eyes.

"Why?" Elvis sighed rhetorically. His eyes misted slightly. He leaned back against the brick wall and tucked his knees under his chest. After an eternity he looked at me with an air of resignation.

"All right, you deserve it." He held up a hand.

"I want to tell you my story, but you have to understand my curiosity about a certain aspect of your story, simply because it so closely involves my family."

"Sure, what is it?"

"How did the judge rule on my money, you know, the estate's money…the royalties…my royalties…you know."

"Oh yeah, I need to tell you what happened," I exclaimed. That is the best part of the story! You know how I told you that it was Giorgio Enricci who was behind Winston Doyle's actions."

Elvis nodded in understanding.

"Well, the short Italian supposedly had a heart attack after he heard that your casket was empty."

Elvis laughed. "You're kidding?"

"And Winston Doyle."

"Yeah, Doc, what about him?"

"He was found hanged with one of his own neck ties."

"Did he commit suicide?"

"Elvis, who knows, because the Enricci family never got the money back."

"Good!"

"And listen to this, Elvis. The judge ruled later that since your body was not found, your estate could control the money as before, with Priscilla still in control. Even though everybody involved in the whole thing was sworn to secrecy, rumors flew about what had happened. Apparently, DELTA Records offered a $2 million reward to the person who could find your whereabouts, supposedly in response to the rumors of your being alive."

"That's actually one of the main reasons I started this..." My voice trailed off. I looked at him and smiled but sternly demanded, "Elvis, I've been telling you this story for two weeks, walking on eggshells. Now it's your turn to clue me in on some of your reasons. You promised!"

I wasn't mad, but I wanted him to tell me as much as he would. I felt like an old woman going on and on about her grandchildren. I was ready for him to tell me something I was dying to hear.

"You explain it to me. Why?"

He hesitated a little, then he started.

"Have you ever thought about how it must have felt to be Elvis Presley, the king of rock 'n' roll?"

Elvis Is Alive

Before I could answer he interrupted. "Sure, it was fun at first. No, it was great, fabulous."

All of a sudden his face turned sad. It was amazing how his expression had changed so quickly when he began to tell me how unhappy he had become. It made me fell sorry again that I was the one making him relive this, but it was time for us to cross that bridge now in our discussion.

He looked me straight in the eye, his voice rising an octave or two. "Look at the way I appeared before I died."

Before I could say anything, Elvis jumped up and went inside the house. He returned and plopped down against the wall again. He produced a large glossy photo of himself when he was his largest. He looked awful. He was bloated, sweating profusely, and was at least fifty pounds overweight.

"See! Look at me now!"

I took the photo and then looked closely at the slim, fit, young-looking man sitting across from me. There was no comparison.

"I was miserable," he exploded.

"Look at me!" he yelled as he pulled the photo from my hand and shook the picture in front of my eyes so I could get a clear view. He was right. He looked ten years younger now and he was twenty years older.

"If something hadn't changed, I would have died," he stated emphatically.

As a physician, I couldn't disagree with him.

He took the photo and looked at it. His expression changed. Maybe it was the shock of seeing how he had looked and the realization of what would have happened if he had not done something. He brightened up.

"But I must confess now," he shyly looked up from the photo at me, "part of that was the plan, to be so bloated my body could be mimicked with a double in the casket. It was mostly from the drugs, but I looked horrible, and I felt it."

"It was a terrible thing to do, but I couldn't stand the prison I was sentenced to. Actually, I made the decision slowly over the years and I finally decided to do it."

I interrupted. "Just like that."

I snapped my fingers. I had gotten to know him well enough that I could talk to him like the friend that he had become.

"You walked away from a type of life that most men dream of living."

He slowly nodded his head in agreement.

"You would have to have lived it to understand," he said. "Besides, Priscilla and I were never going to get back together."

I looked at him and stared. I couldn't believe it. The most popular entertainer in the world just up and leaves his home, family, friends and fans just because he didn't want to be Elvis Presley anymore. I was expecting some fantastic story about the Mafia, debts...anything but this.

"How exactly did you pull it off?"

Elvis smiled at that. "I can't tell you everything because, to be honest, I don't remember everything. Afterall, it has been twenty years and...the drugs..." his voice trailed off.

I nodded my head, attempting to show that I understood that it might not be possible to recall everything.

"Well, Dr. St. John, it was easier than you might think. My family doctor gave me a dose of beta blockers and, that stuff..." he squinched his forehead trying to remember. "You know that stuff they give you when they put you to sleep in surgery."

"You're kidding?" I asked incredulously. But then I shook my head as I thought, *Yeah, that might do it.* I was amazed that he risked taking those kinds of drugs.

"It really wasn't as hard as you might think!"

Elvis scooted back to fit in tighter against the brick wall. I don't know what he was thinking, but this was definitely anticlimactic. I guess I had searched for him so long and spent so much time trying to find him that it was disquieting to be told that it was easy to pull it off. How could he have fooled all of those people?

"How did you find me in Paris? When you called me that night, how did you get my telephone number?" he asked.

"Detective work!" It was my time to be coy. "Elvis, why don't we wait until tomorrow. It will give you time to see if you can recall more of the details. I'm beat."

"Fair enough," he agreed.

By now it had become much darker. The girls had already gone to bed. Elvis and I sat alone in the garden. Pierre was still rummaging around in the kitchen, as it was his habit to stay up until Elvis went to sleep.

We continued to drink the strong aromatic coffee. It seemed as if we had become addicted to it, or maybe, we had just become used to drinking it as we talked.

Silently we stared up at the stars in the French sky. I couldn't resist one last question that night.

"So you just decided to leave everything and go live a new life?"

He didn't answer other than to look at me and nod his head in the affirmative. He waited at least five minutes before he said anything else.

"Good coffee, isn't it?" He held his cup up for me to inspect.

"Yeah."

Elvis then sighed a very deep and wistful sigh. He looked at me straight in the eye.

"Dr. St. John, there's no way anyone could understand. No one else has been raised up from the delta of rural Mississippi and then been proclaimed a "King," except me. It's something that no one else could possibly comprehend." He smiled that quirky smile of his, with that smirk on his lip.

Suddenly everything was okay. I no longer felt so…stupid. For the past year there had been a great void in my life. This adventure had consumed me. It had become an obsession. Even though I had expected some kind of startling revelation—a terminal illness that had been miraculously cured or something that dramatic, his reason for doing what he did now filled that void in my life. His reasoning seemed inconsequential. I could now return to Memphis in peace. My mission was mostly accomplished. I realized it was he who had lost so much, not I. Yet he had made the decision, and he would have to live with it.

"Have you ever thought about going back?" I blurted out.

He looked at me in a strange way.

"Yeah, I've thought about it. If I didn't have Babette, it's something that I would actually consider. But you know…" His face suddenly turned sad again.

"That's something that I knew when I made this decision that could probably never be done, go back."

"I guess not," I agreed.

"Hey, I've got another question." His face lit up again. "How exactly did you find me? I mean how did you trace me to Paris."

"Magic!" I teased. I was tired, and that part of the story was probably best told at another time. Maybe I would even write a letter to him from home and explain that part of my trip, it was so complicated.

"Hey, why haven't you performed since we've been back?" I asked, changing the subject.

The smile returned to his face as he began, "I have a fill-in. He's entertaining there this week in my place. Hey, why don't we take the girls to the Moulin Rouge tomorrow night?"

"Okay Elvis, I'd like that. But then I need to get back to the good old U.S.A. I'll stay one more day, then I'll head home."

Elvis tried to talk me into staying for another week or so, "I'm certain I can remember everything!" he offered. "Dr. St. John, you've been so patient. I'm positive I will recall everything that happened if I sit down with you and really concentrate. So why don't you stick around for a few more days."

It was nice to know that he wanted me to stay, but I had made up my mind. It was time to go home.

"I've got another day, Elvis. Hopefully you can remember everything before I go. If not, I promise to try and come back."

Robert Mickey Maughon, M.D.

"Okay, If it's time to go, I understand," was all Elvis said.

To be honest, I'm not sure if he really wanted to tell me everything or not. But I wasn't upset by his dancing around his story because I had had such a good time being his guest.

After a few minutes of silence, he looked at me, "Let's go on to bed."

With that, we both got up and headed off to sleep.

Chapter Twenty-Four

It was going to be sad heading back to the U.S. This part of my life was over. I had not given up until I had found out most of the truth. Now I knew the majority of it. Who knows if I would ever learn all of the details of Elvis' incredible story .The part of the story that he had related to me seemed so simple. I guess that's just the way it is sometimes. Something that should be so complicated comes down to a very simple explanation.

Would I do this over again? Spend so much time devoted to the chase? Yes, I guess I would. No, I know I would. I'm just so stubborn sometimes. This episode happened to be one of those times.

That night I settled into bed next to Brigitte. Her warm, moist lips met mine and we made love. The last thing I remember before I drifted off to sleep was the sweet aroma of her breath on my face. Yeah, this journey had definitely been worth the trouble, I decided as I fell asleep.

The next morning greeted me with an unexpected sadness. I felt remorseful in a way. I had made such good friends. I wished Brigitte lived in the U.S., considering what had happened between Marcia and me. I determined that I was

Robert Mickey Maughon, M.D.

going to ask Brigitte to come back stateside with me. It seemed sudden, but what the heck? Maybe she wanted to see the U.S.

Even Pierre seemed somewhat down as I met him in the kitchen. He must have known that day was going to be my last in Paris. I don't know if Elvis had told him or he had an innate feel for my leaving. It seems as if he had a special gift for that kind of thing.

I had always wanted to go to the Moulin Rouge. During my time in Paris, the only sightseeing I had done was the trip to the Eiffel Tower. I guess the tourist stuff would have to wait until my next visit.

Babette and Brigitte came downstairs together. Brigitte ran over to me and hugged my neck. She was speaking rapidly in French. Elvis had evidently told Babette I was going home and she had told Brigitte. I blurted out that I wanted Brigitte to come back with me as I kissed her.

She kept saying *"non"* as she kissed me, hugging me tightly around the neck.

The day passed quickly. I made reservations to fly back on the Concorde. I was ready to go home and that was the fastest way to get there. Elvis said nothing about the rest of his story. Either he couldn't remember or it was going to be too painful to try. Either way, I was his close friend now and it just didn't seem to matter much to me either way.

We dressed up to go to the show. The girls looked fabulous. I must admit that Elvis and I looked great also. He was particularly handsome in his Armani tuxedo. As we were both approximately the same size, I borrowed another

Elvis Is Alive

tux from him. It felt great dressing up and going out with my new friends. Imagine, a night on the town in Paris with Elvis Presley. It was a great going-away present.

As we approached the Moulin Rouge, a young tourist from America ran up to Elvis. She started to jump up and down, exclaiming that he was Elvis Presley. He calmly explained that he was an impersonator and had a show in town. He handed her a free pass to the Elvis Review. She took it and glumly walked away, obviously disappointed. He looked over at me and winked. "See, it works every time."

The show at the Moulin Rouge was marvelous. I've never seen such perfect legs on a group of ladies. Elvis and I had to feign disinterest as the near-naked female bodies danced around seductively in front of us.

Babette and Brigitte were looking at us constantly to see how closely we were taking in the scenery. That was some of the best acting I've ever done, trying to not look at a bunch of beautiful, nearly naked girls.

When we left the show, Elvis and I both had to frown and pretend that the show was just okay. We both made faces of indifference. We didn't fool the girls at all as they playfully hugged us as we headed back to Elvis' home.

We were walking through a block of fashionable boutiques when the girls stopped behind to look at some of the new Paris fashions.

Elvis and I had continued to walk ahead, talking. One minute, we were looking back at the girls telling them to hurry up. The next minute, they were gone, lost in the rubble of a huge explosion that rocked the whole block. What had been a happy scene with people walking through the street enjoying the night became a horrible nightmare. We rushed to the storefront where just seconds before the girls had been standing, admiring the new clothes.

We picked and clawed through the rubble. Sirens began to scream from everywhere. Another tranquil Paris evening had been shattered by a terrorist's blast.

Four people were killed that night due to the explosion. Ten more innocent human beings were seriously injured. We reached Babette and Brigitte as quickly as was humanly possible, but it was too late. Nothing could be done. I have never seen a man weep as hard as Elvis Presley did that night as he knelt in the rubble, clutching the lifeless body of Babette tightly to his chest.

I held up until the funeral two days later. I then joined him in weeping at the horror of losing two so young to such a random and wicked act.

The four of us had no political feelings. Yet our lives were ripped asunder by some religious zealot who cared not one whit about human life. I don't remember too much about the funeral or the bereaved families of the two girls. To be honest, I don't remember much about the rest of my time in Paris.

I canceled my flight home until three days after the funerals. Pierre consoled Elvis as much as possible, but it didn't seem to help much. For some reason, I felt responsible. If I hadn't found him, we wouldn't have been in front of that shop that night. On and on my reasoning went. It was not my fault, I know, but I still felt guilty.

Elvis Is Alive

Of course, I still had questions of how he had pulled it off, exactly. I knew Elvis had not told me everything. Now, I surmised, I would probably never know. I didn't bring up the subject to him at all because, strangely, I didn't want to know. It would remind me too much that without my presence in Paris, Babette and Brigitte might still be alive.

The afternoon of the night I was to leave, Elvis disappeared. I had a 10 p.m. flight to New York on the Concorde.

Pierre told me not to worry as he helped me pack. He said Elvis wanted me to meet him at the small bar where he and I had first met. I was emotional as I hugged Pierre before I left. I felt as if he would always be a good friend of mine. Pierre arranged a taxi for me and gave the driver instructions. In broken English, he asked me to "hurry back."

The mist had begun to swirl up from the Seine as I entered the bar. Even though there were a few people milling around outside, the only person in the place, besides the same old bartender, was Elvis.

We sat at the same table where we had first met. I could feel that the deaths of Brigitte and Babette had made us closer in a "brotherly" sort of way. I don't recall a lot of what Elvis said, it was all such a blur.

But when I asked him if he was going to stay in Paris, he shrugged his shoulders and said, "Probably not."

I do remember asking him if he would return to his former life.

He matter of factly said, "I doubt it."

He then reached over and grabbed my hand, opening my palm. He dropped a small ring with a garnet stone and diamond into it. I protested that he could not give me such a nice gift.

He said simply that it had been a gift for someone who was "very close." Perhaps it was going to be an engagement ring for Babette. Anyway, his generosity had been legendary, and he had not lost it.

"Read the inscription," he said, pointing to the ring. "That's where I was this afternoon, at the jeweler's."

On the inside of the band was delicately inscribed, "Dr. St. John, remember Paris and me, E.P."

We didn't have a whole lot more to say. Besides, I was afraid I would break down and cry. We hugged on the outside, just as I was getting back into the cab.

As we broke our embrace, he patted me on the shoulder and said simply, "Good-bye."

I looked out the rear window of the small yellow taxi as we drove away. The last I saw of Elvis, he was walking down that Paris street, disappearing into the swirling, misty fog.

OTHER NOVELS BY

ROBERT MICKEY MAUGHON, M.D.

BellWitch:The Movie   ISBN # 0-9765141-0-9

New Orleans E R   ISBN # 0-96-50366-0-X

Amazon.com

BarnesandNoble.com

BellWitchthemovie.com